What Goes Around
COMES AROUND

PARANORMAL MYSTERY

Contemporary Romance

Geek to Chic
Honeymoon Husband
Just Like Jack

Contemporary Holiday Romance

Christmas is a-Coming

Paranormal

What Goes Around - Comes Around
(Contemporary Ghost Mystery)

Portrait of Lady Margaret
(Regency Time Travel)

ISBN-13: 978-1-946314-00-0 (paperback)

ISBN-10: 1-946314-00-5

ISBN-13: 978-1-94314-01-7 (ebook)

ISBN-10: 1-946314-01-3

Photographs provided by Unsplashed.com

Photographers:

Jordane Mathieu - background

Fernando Aguilar - knife

Sarah Gotzo - back

www.ShirleyMarks.com

To my sisters

the spe is leaving the station

.

What Goes Around
COMES AROUND

PARANORMAL MYSTERY

SHIRLEY MARKS

1

NATALIE POWELL THOUGHT her sister was talking about breakfast when she said, "Hot, sweet, firm buns," and not a man.

This proved that eight-thirty in the morning was too early for her to be around people. Normally, Nat would be in bed, buried deep under her toasty covers trying to make up for her usual three a.m. bedtime by sleeping until ten.

But not today. Nat rubbed her neck and shuffled in line toward the counter of the crowded Starbucks. She preferred the Blue Sky Café with its slightly tacky every-shade-of-blue décor, good food, and, in her opinion, even better coffee. Still, the aroma of freshly ground beans filled the air.

Caffeine wasn't the reason she'd come to the trendy coffee house. As a common pairing, Starbucks and one of the last few remaining Barnes & Noble, where Becca worked, sat side by side. Meeting here was convenient for them both, Nat was there to pick up the keys to Rebecca's car and Becca had a major crush on one of the coffee dispensers, Theo.

At Becca's urging, Nat stepped up to the counter and placed her order. She stifled a yawn and pointed into the refrigerated food case. "I'll have the chocolate, cream cheese croissant and a double whipped, quad-cappuccino."

"There he is, over there, at the espresso machine." Becca nudged Nat and glanced in Theo's direction.

A tall aproned fellow with dark hair, up in a man-bun, glanced in their direction. Nat guessed he was suppressing a smile, but the way he kept looking at her showed he definitely had eyes for her sister.

"Are you two together?" The cashier snagged a to-go cup and marked Nat's order on its side with a black Sharpie then turned her attention to Becca.

"Ah—sure." Becca shrugged and held out her Starbucks card to the cashier. "I'll have a small decaf latte."

"And the luscious man-body behind the machine," Nat whispered for only Becca to hear.

"Shut up," Becca hushed Nat and elbowed her as a subtle warning.

"Small decaf latte," the barista repeated and punched the order into the cash register before swinging into the refrigerated pastry case. He used a pair of tongs, slid a chocolate cream cheese croissant into a bag and set it on the counter. "What's the name on that?"

"Becca."

The cashier marked a second cup with Becca's name and drink order before announcing the total cost. "How would you like to pay for this?"

Becca held out a plastic card.

"I'll take the total off your Starbucks' card, then." The card was swiped and returned in a quick, efficient manner. "Would you like a receipt today?"

"No, that's fine." Nat took the card—Becca was too busy staring at Theo—and pushed her sister out of the growing order line to make room for the other patrons.

"Extra caffeine and a double dose of fat? What's the occasion?" Becca managed, asking Nat between glances in Theo's direction.

"Number one: Because I work the late shift at the restaurant so I don't usually get up this early and two: I'm about to interview for a job I desperately want and hope that my desperation doesn't show."

"Small decaf latte for Becca," Theo called out from the order pick-up area.

"That's mine." Becca, anxious to be by her man's side, raced for Theo in a near dead-run.

"Yeah, you wish." Nat couldn't help mumbling. "I'll try and grab us a spot." She snagged a table for two against the window just as someone stepped away from one of the remaining few, if not the only empty place to sit.

"Hi, Theo," Becca said in her best ask-me-out-you-fool voice.

"Good morning, Becca." His voice was probably smoother than the coffee.

Oh, yes. There was no doubt about it, this had to be true love. Nat felt as if she'd been pushed onto the back burner to simmer. It would be only a minute until Mr. Wonderful would have to get back to work and Nat could have Becca's semi-divided attention.

He said a quick something that Nat couldn't make out and Becca's smile widened.

"Double whipped, quad-cappuccino," Theo's co-worker announced.

Becca waved at Nat that she'd pick up her drink. And that gave her a chance to stand there and talk longer to the apple of her eye.

"Well?" Nat prompted when Becca sat at the table.

"His shift ends at two and he says he'll come by to see me." Becca slid Nat's cappuccino to her then glanced at Theo. "I think he's going to ask me out."

"Finally. You've only been talking about him for two months."

"But he didn't notice me the first six weeks. I guess he thought

I was just another steady customer. Then he told me the benefits of having a Starbucks card."

"That's definitely life-altering," Nat commented, mostly to herself she picked up the spoon and stirred her hot drink, trying to cool it down a bit before taking her first sip.

"I don't see guys lining up to meet you." Becca glanced from Nat's flaky, chocolate pastry to her beverage, piled high with whipped cream. "No guy's gonna even look at you if you keep eating that way."

"Hey—there's more to life than men, you know." Nat narrowed her eyes and couldn't help but feel a little defensive.

Men weren't everything. And Nat kept her mouth shut, she didn't want to argue. Not here, not now, especially when she was there for a favor.

Becca leaned back in her seat. "Please, not the *career speech* again."

"Well, you know how it is." Nat shrugged. "I like men just fine but I don't look like you."

Cute and thin. That had never been Nat.

Nat was attractive-in-a-different-kind-of-way from her sister and had always been considered of having the "nice personality." It didn't matter, any dating and all man choices were a disaster. She was much better off with a sauté pan and a stainless steel whisk.

"I can't plan that I'll ever meet anyone. It may never happen for me but that's okay. I've got my own plans for my future."

"I know. You've told me a hundred times—your future's in the kitchen." Becca rocked her head from side to side, punctuating every other word.

"I can't help it. I love cooking... and baking. *Love* it." Nat uttered in the same enthusiastic tone as Becca had told her about Theo.

"Uncle, okay?" Becca held up her hands in surrender and took a cleansing breath. "Can we backtrack a sec? What did you say about your job? You're looking for a new one, right? Did you get fired?"

"I did not get fired. Weren't you listening?" Obviously, she hadn't been. Becca only had eyes and ears, it seemed, for her current crush, Theo. "I said I'm interviewing for a job at Side Street Sam's."

"And you already have a job at the Bistro? Didn't they just promote you two months ago?"

She made Nat sound a little ungrateful and scheming, enacting the grass is greener scenario. Nat wasn't so much greedy, wanting another job while she already had one, as she was ambitious and wanted to climb the kitchen staff ladder. Was it such a crime to want a little independence? Or to want to get ahead?

"Sam's is looking now. It'd be a full-on fantasy to work there. It doesn't have to be a better position. If I'm hired as an assistant to the pasta chef or even to the sauté cook, it's all good. A lateral move from 3rd Street Bistro to Side Street Sam's is a move up."

"Okay. So you're in the midst of this pivotal career move and you have a big interview all lined up." Becca sipped her coffee and eyed Nat with only the slightest interest she'd given Theo. "You're not planning to go in looking like that, are you?"

Nat looked down at her comfortable baggy, gray-colored Henley, hanging mid-thigh over her navy blue sweatpants and shook her head. "Give me a break, I just got up. I plan on changing my clothes before I interview."

"That's good to hear. The only job you'll get dressed like that is with the kitchen clean-up crew."

Fingering her short, unruly hair, that sort of stuck out in all directions because it wasn't being held under a chef's hat. Nat wondered if she really looked all that bad and, in a bout of self-doubt, tried to smooth her hair down. She'd make herself look presentable. She was more than capable when it came to cooking and that's what really mattered.

Becca glanced at her wristwatch. "I've got to get going. I don't want to be fired for being late." She took a last sip of her coffee before she pushed the half-filled cup toward Nat, and stood. "I'm not even close to having another job lined up—unlike some people."

"Nothing is for certain." Nat caught Becca's eye roll. "It's just an interview."

"Oh, I almost forgot. Here you go." Becca handed the key fob for her car to Nat. "Just remember to park in the employee section when you get back."

"I will." Nat nodded.

"And don't forget to put up the sunshade."

"I won't." Nat shook her head.

"Good luck today, okay?" Becca flashed a smile. "I hope you know what you're doing."

Just for the record, Nat did, too.

SIDE STREET SAM'S office was located in the Samuel Whitaker Hotel in San Francisco's Union Square. Nat thought about the daily commute she'd have to make. Much farther than her short walk from the San Bruno apartment she shared with Becca. They'd end up car-sharing for a while or maybe she'd take the train but it would be worth it in the long run.

Nat readjusted her black tailored pin-striped jacket over her crisp white dress shirt and ran her hand down her thigh, smoothing her slacks out of nervousness. She'd taken extra care to tame her short, shorn locks, making certain they didn't give her any problems. She did not want any reason to feel insecure today. The receptionist told her to go into the office and have a seat.

Walking into the room, Nat pulled the door closed behind her and took in the heavy antique furniture inside the high-ceilinged room. A single chair faced a large, ornate desk. The chair, Nat guessed, was for her. The three chairs on the opposite side of the desk were for her "interrogators."

On a round table in front of her stood a four foot high sparkling crystal vase. Lit with a small spotlight from above, this year's International Culinary Competition, Division 52 trophy was proudly located in the center of the room, shouting its importance.

Impressive.

Oh, yeah, Nat would love to be a part of that.

Some day.

She walked around the table and eased into the chair, facing the massive, solid-looking, carved desk. How long would she have to wait? Nat was doing her best to keep her nerves in check. But how long could she do it? Hopefully, until the end of the interview.

Glancing around at her surroundings, Nat felt dwarfed by the high-ceilinged room. She could tell this place was old; probably built or reconstructed shortly after the 1906 Earthquake as many of the buildings in the city had been.

A side door opened and in walked a stocky man in a dark double-breasted suit, Lawrence Kaster, Sam's operations manager. A second man followed. He wore a chef's white slacks and jacket with dark blue piping, Angelo Dimico, the restaurant's executive chef.

Finally, a third man entered. Dressed in crisp white chef's garb and a black baseball cap with Sam's written in a white script, he stepped into the room and pulled the door closed behind him.

It had been a good five years and his once full-beard was now trimmed down to a tidy goatee, giving him the impression of a dark and sinister character one wouldn't want to bump into in an alley.

Nat recognized him immediately. Daine Owens.... he must now be a sous chef. Sam's sous chef.

Nat blinked then swallowed. Talk about rotten luck. This was the worst.

Why did he have to be here?

She might as well kiss this job goodbye. Chef Dimico might be the man to impress but Owens would be the man Nat would have to work alongside every day. And Nat knew he'd never have her in his kitchen again.

He wasn't a pleasure to work with when he was a line-cook and she the lowly apprentice. She was chopping, running around, doing grunge work. He was yelling out orders, bossing people around, and causing major terror among the lower staff members. He'd be even worse with more of a swelled head now that he was second-in-command of the kitchen.

Amazed that he could find a beanie to fit his head, Nat wondered if he had any hair and that was why he covered his head. Probably thinning or bald she thought to herself.

Well, this interview was over before it started. Sometimes you win, sometimes you lose. Maybe she should just back out altogether. The next hour, or two, was going to be torture and Nat couldn't wait until this was over so she could high-tail it out of there and back to the safety of her steady job.

THIS PLACE LOOKED the same as all the places had looked at first. Gray, indistinct, and gloomy but it wouldn't stay that way for long. Sometimes one was alone, sometimes there were others, but one never knew.

This time there was a man with light brown, curly hair. The other man was slightly taller and more muscular. His hair was dark brown, swept back from his forehead, and his chin had a deep cleft.

"Hi, there," the light-haired man said.

"Howdy," the dark-haired man said.

"Simon. 1985."

"Mitch. 1948."

That's all they needed: a name and a date, the year they departed. A long silence stretched out between the two men after their brief but adequate introductions. Both understood what it meant.

"Where is this place?" Simon shifted his attention from his companion to their hazy surroundings.

"I dunno." Mitch, the more adventurous of the two, stepped out, scouting the boundaries.

"I don't know what to make of this. Reminds me of... of... something... I don't remember." Simon who always liked to label every person and place found this unsettling. "Come to think of it, everything's pretty fuzzy."

Simon wouldn't let Mitch out of his sight until their surroundings cleared up. A moment later, a heavy round table appeared a few feet from them. They drifted toward the table, on it sat a dramatically lit tall cut crystal vase.

International Culinary Competition, Division 52, was the inscription on the base.

"Why do I always have to be in this monkey suit?" Mitch unbuttoned his jacket and pulled at his wide necktie, loosening it.

"They wanted you to look your best, I'm sure. In 1948 it was probably the height of fashion." Simon adjusted the lapel around his white stand-up collar and made sure the ends of his cashmere scarf, artfully draped around his neck, hung even. He nodded in approval at the cuffs on his trousers and the condition of his platform shoes.

"I doubt it. It was probably something they pulled out from

the back of an old wardrobe." Mitch pulled the short-brimmed hat from his head and tossed it to the side, not caring where it landed. "That is a dog-ugly hat. I think someone was trying to get back at me."

Simon pulled at the erect collar on his white shirt and straightened the sleeves of his blazer. "I've always liked this outfit."

"Pick out the duds yourself, did you?"

"Why, yes, I did." Simon flashed a wide smile, displaying an amazing amount of white, straight teeth. "I used to be—"

Mitch held up his hand silencing Simon. "Did you hear that? I don't think we're the only ones here."

"The only ones except for her." Simon pointed at the young lady in the pin-striped black jacket, sitting in a chair. "Shhh. Careful, she might be able to hear you."

Funny how they hadn't seen her only moments before. She must have been there the whole time and was only now sliding into their reality.

A smile spread over Mitch's lips. "Now she's a looker. Take that suit off her and I wouldn't mind sticking around. Maybe we could—"

"Hold on there, Casanova. Don't you know any better?" Simon stretched his arm out, blocking Mitch. "She's off-limits."

HOURS LATER AFTER her disastrous interview, Nat glanced beyond the bill of her black baseball hat uniform at her co-workers who wore the same. They were all good people, capable, and fun to work with. She really would miss them when it was time to move on to a new job—whenever that time came.

Thinking back to that morning, Nat decided that it hadn't been a complete waste of time. Handling the pressure and answering the questions had been good practice. She wasn't going to get that job, not in a million years, with Daine Owens on the panel.

As she recalled, he'd been unreasonable and a complete tyrant, riding nearly everyone's back in the kitchen. He could give Gordon Ramsey a run for his money.

No, life at the 3rd Street Bistro was nothing to complain about and with her recent promotion, Nat wasn't doing half bad. With the exception of running into Owens, life was treating her pretty good.

"Service has all gone home," Randy Ellis, the sous chef, announced, coming into the kitchen. "How you doing, Sasha?"

"Just about finished." Sasha made the last few swipes with her rag, drying the well-used grill for the night.

"Got the greens list for tomorrow?" Ellis called through the shelves at Matthew the pantry cook.

"Done," Matthew responded. "Ready to go over changes for tomorrow night's menu."

"Be right there," Ellis answered. "Powell?"

"Finished, sir." Nat had just cleaned up her area and deposited the rags in the laundry hamper.

"Then what are you doing hanging around?" He motioned for her to go home.

No one had to tell her twice.

She untied her apron and folded it before tossing it on the pile with the rest of the soiled linens. On her way to her locker, Nat glanced out the open kitchen door and saw two men in a booth near the restaurant's entrance.

"Didn't service go home?" She stood with her hands on her hips. "Why are there still patrons here?"

Sasha sidled up to her and gave the dining room a once over. She glanced at Nat, shrugged, and walked away.

Oh, no. This wasn't right. Nat said to herself about the two gentlemen sitting in a booth.

Hadn't someone given them the last call? It was after two a.m. and Nat was awfully tired.

No one was supposed to be in the restaurant. It should have been completely empty.

The two gentlemen were nicely dressed in odd-looking suits, both nursed drinks. They weren't talking or laughing like they were having a good time. It looked to Nat as if they were waiting.

But waiting for what? Or who?

She was hesitant to approach them herself. It wasn't her job but everyone working in front had gone and no one, except her, from the back, seemed to know these two were here. Someone had to take the initiative.

"THERE SHE IS again," Simon alerted Mitch who glanced up when the kitchen doors swung open, then he went back to staring at his drink. "You see her, don't you?"

"Yup." Mitch concentrated on the rim of his glass.

"She's one of us, right?"

"I dunno." He slid his glass back and forth in a shallow motion, clinking the ice cubes from one side to the other. "Did you see her talking to someone else?"

Simon pulled his attention away from Mitch and took his time studying the young lady. "We'll have to be extra careful then."

"You got it." Mitch sipped his drink and frowned. "It just doesn't taste the same."

"So tell me your story." Simon settled back into the seat, making himself comfortable.

"It's a long one."

"I think we've got some time to kill." Simon glanced upward and shrugged. "Shoot."

Mitch jumped.

"A little sensitive, are we? I guess I hit a nerve." Simon felt another jolt when he said the word *hit*. "Oooh... sorry, didn't mean to say that either. I must have done it again. Go on talk, I'm listening."

"Not much to tell. I grew up in Crawford, Ohio and was a gunner in the war."

"Nam, huh?" Simon could sympathize completely. He hadn't served but he knew a lot of men who had gone to Vietnam.

"*World War II*. I was stationed in England. Polebrook." Mitch glanced at Simon incredulously. "After the war, a captain-buddy of mine said I had a nice looking mug and I should head to California, Hollywood to make movies after I got home."

"A captain?" Simon perked up, sounding interested in what Mitch had to say.

Mug? As in *mug*-shot?

"Did he have any connections in the business?" Simon seemed a little star struck at the mention of the glitz and glamour of the film industry.

"The King said he was ready to abdicate and I was perfect to take his place."

"The King of England?" Simon gasped, wide-eyed.

"Of Hollywood."

"You knew Elvis?" Simon gushed, even wider-eyed.

Mitch arched his eyebrow and leaned forward. "*Clark Gable*."

Nat had given them more than enough time. Hadn't they noticed the empty tables and booths around them? The lack of wait-staff? She took her time and strolled over to the booth.

"Excuse me, gentlemen. We're closed and you're going to have to leave."

"Anything you say, toots," the dark-haired one said.

"We're ready if you are," the curly-haired one replied.

Nat picked up their glasses, walked to the bar, and set them on the counter. She moved her hands away and stared.

They were different. The glasses. One was a heavy-based rocks glass. The other a multi-colored martini glass. Neither of them belonged to this restaurant.

She pivoted to take another look at the men.

They were gone. The booth they had occupied, empty.

Swinging her gaze to the front of the restaurant, she wondered how they had managed to exit so quickly when someone would have had to unlock the front door to let them out.

Nat turned back to the bar. The empty glasses were gone.

2

I THINK THEY'RE following me.

Nat caught the reflection of the two men in the glass of the Starbucks' pastry display case the next morning. They looked to her to be the same two men she'd kicked out of the restaurant last night.

But that was crazy. Why would they be following her?

"We'll have the morning commute up in a few minutes but first, we have a tragic story of the death of a young, local heiress. Georgette..." the wall-mounted, flat-screen television broadcasted the morning newscast.

Nat looked over her shoulder to check and see if those two men were still there. There they were, standing outside next to the tree. And if she weren't mistaken, they were dressed the same as they had been the last time she'd seen them.

"Becca, do you see those guys?" Nat stared at the light-haired man who wore a dark blazer over his white shirt and bright red-colored vest. The other guy looked like he'd stepped out of some old-time black and white movie.

Of course Becca hadn't seen them. She only saw Theo who was now returning her goo-goo eyes.

"Thank you, Ron. Local Bay Area heiress Georgette Price was found dead this morning in her home. Ms. Price was the daughter of the self-made millionaire George Victor Price who made his fortune in the 1960s...."

"Look out there. By the tree, on the other side of the newspaper stands. You see them?"

Becca finally pulled her attention away from Theo and glanced out the window. "I don't see anyone."

"No one?" Nat glanced at the tree again. There was no one there. "I was just making sure." Okay, so maybe Becca didn't see them but Nat strongly suspected they *were* following her.

"Oh, Nat. He's perfect," Becca whispered with a sigh.

"They all are." Nat wondered where her two shadows had gone.

"What?"

"Nothing." Just a personal commentary on Becca's men. They're always perfect until she found the chink in their armor, then they turned to be only some guy wearing a trash can. "Did you and Theo hook up yesterday after his shift?"

"He came over and we stood by the Horror and Mystery book section, just talking, and he asked me out. I met him by the Magazine Section after work and then we took a long walk and after that, we stopped for some pizza. We spent nearly all night talking. He's wonderful."

"...The police won't comment on the details of her death. She was just twenty years old."

"It must have gone well at your interview yesterday. That's why you need to borrow my car again today, right?" Becca spoke to Nat but kept glancing at Theo.

"I guess they liked me. I got a phone call this morning. They're having a lunch for three of the candidates this afternoon. But it doesn't matter, there's no way they're going to hire me."

"Oh, come on. That's not the confident little sister I know. You're gonna get the job."

"No, I won't. Management may like me but they don't have the final say on who gets hired." Nat knew how kitchen politics worked. "I guess it isn't well-known but do you know who the sous chef is at Side Street Sam's?" Of course, Becca would have no idea. "Daine Owens."

"Why does that name sound familiar?" Becca might not be up on who's who in the cooking world and it wasn't likely that the name Daine Owens ever came up.

"I interned with him at—"

"Oh, yeah. I remember you talking about that guy. You hated him." Nat was astonished that Becca had managed to pull her attention from Theo to retrieve a little something from her memory. "You really hated him."

"Even if I somehow got the job... I could make it work." Maybe. "I'm a professional." Definitely. "It doesn't matter that he's a self-centered crockpot."

"If anyone could do it, you can." Becca checked her wrist-watch. "I've got to get going. Here you go." She handed over the key fob to her car. "See ya, have a good time. Think positive, okay? You got this!" She stood and blew a kiss to Theo who caught it and plastered it on his cheek then returned a smile.

Those two were just too cute for words.

Nat had to get going, too. Things to do. Get home, get ready, and get on the road. She dropped her empty cup in the trash and headed for the door. Pausing before she stepped outside, Nat glanced around looking—just looking. Not a trace of those two guys.

It was safe.

As she walked down the street, Nat kept a careful watch all the way to the parking lot.

"Excuse me, I'm sorry to bother you."

Nat spun around. He was there—they were there—both of them—like out of nowhere, standing right next to her.

"Could we speak to you for a minute?" The curly, light-haired man moved toward her.

"Look, you guys—take my purse." Nat held it out for them. She wasn't going to put up a fight for the five bucks in her wallet.

"We don't want your purse." He held his hands up in a display of nonviolence.

"Just leave me alone, okay?" She dropped it and moved back, bumping up against the car.

The dark-haired guy slid his hat onto the hood and turned his attention to Nat. "We're not going to hurt you, *doll*." He acted as if he did this all the time.

Yeah, she felt scared but she believed him. Nat nearly melted into a puddle where she stood when the dark-haired man smiled at her. Talk about turning on the charm, this man reeked of *man-gnetism.*

"So what do you want?" This felt weird. Facing her stalkers was unexplainably creepy, she should have been terrified but she wasn't. Nat should have been screaming her lungs out, calling for help. But she didn't.

"Just an introduction," Mr. Charisma said.

"This is Mitch Hudson and I'm Simon Dijon" —the curly-haired man indicated with a flourish— "Like the mustard."

"Natalie Powell." Nat reached out to shake Simon's hand and hers passed right through his.

"LIKE THE MUSTARD," Mitch mimicked, making fun of Simon's last words. He glanced around at his surroundings and didn't give a thought to the small urban area—an overstuffed floral

chair, an old green davenport, and a small round table that matched the coffee table.

"I only wanted to get started off on the right foot, you know." Simon made a calming motion with his hands. "Ease her into all this."

"Well, what are you going to do next? We don't have much time. She's right outside." Mitch jerked his head toward the front door.

"How do you know?" Simon sounded nervous as if he weren't ready for a second try at his first impression.

"If she wasn't there then we wouldn't be here." Mitch walked to the sofa and sat.

"Good point." Simon glanced around and took a few cleansing, calming breaths to pull himself together. "We can try it your way, but don't blame me if we scare the striped bikini briefs off of her."

"You started all this with your *introductions*. That's not the way to start a—"

"*Relationship*?" Simon tactfully interjected.

"Sure, bud. Call it whatever you want. We gotta get started if we ever want to make any progress." Mitch dropped his Trilby hat on the coffee table. "I hate that hat. I wish I never had to see that hat again."

"All right, so I'm not so good at this. It's not as if I've had as much practice as you have."

"What's that supposed to mean?" Mitch was really getting fed up with this guy.

"1948 and 1985... hmm... that's how many years you've got on me?" Simon ticked off his fingers as if he were immersed in some sort of complex mathematical calculation. He shook his hand then threw up his arms, giving up. "All that matters is that you've been around much longer than I. You must have done this at least a dozen times more and yet... you're still here." Simon glared at

Mitch through narrowed eyelids. "Someone must be a little hard-headed, huh? Not learning their lesson?"

"Shut your yap," Mitch said over his shoulder. "No one's asking for your opinion."

"It's not like there's any choice now, is there?" Simon crossed his arms and leaned against the door jam. "Looks like we're stuck in this together, just the two of us."

The deadbolt on the door chunked open and keys jingled at the doorknob.

Mitch glanced from Simon to the door and corrected him, "You'd better make that the three of us."

IT HAD TAKEN Nat all of two seconds to jump in the car, start it up and get the hell out of there.

"I did not see that. I did not see that," she repeated over and over. What she thought happened couldn't have happened. Concentrating on her driving, Nat tried not to think of people appearing out of thin air and seeing transparent type of ghostly flesh.

Those guys had looked solid enough when she was talking to them.

Don't think about it!

All she wanted to do is get home and lock the door behind her.

She popped the deadbolt open and couldn't keep her keys from dancing while she worked on the handle.

Just open the door, already.

Nat stepped inside, closed the door behind her, and threw the lock.

Safe. Finally.

She leaned against the door and let out her breath with her eyes closed, allowing herself to relax.

"We go where you go," a cheery man's voice, Simon's, it turns out said.

Nat screamed and would have jumped away from them except she'd already closed and locked the door behind her. "What the hell are you doing here?"

"Just calm down, okay?" The words held a bit more sincerity coming from Mitch. "You aren't nuts or anything."

Does it make you any less crazy if your delusion is telling you that you haven't lost your mind?

Nat didn't think so.

"Why don't you have a seat?" Mitch stood and stepped aside, gesturing for her to sit on the moss green colored sofa.

Nat moved past Mitch and eased down into the cushion but did not relax. She couldn't. "I don't have time for this. I have to get ready."

"We just want to talk to you, explain what's going on." Simon moved away from her to the overstuffed chair. "It won't take long."

"I haven't got time for this," Nat said in an emotionless ultra-calm voice. "I just don't have time for a nervous breakdown. Not now." She was talking more to herself than she was to them.

"You're not losing your marbles." Simon sat facing her with his hands clasped in his lap.

"But you two aren't real." Two strange... *really* strange... men in her apartment. Again, she should have been scared to death but Nat did not feel threatened.

"Oh, we're real. We're about as real as it gets." Simon chuckled to himself.

"Okay, give it a rest, *Mustard- Boy*. Natalie, we're from the other side," Mitch said simply.

"Of the tracks? Of the world?" Of the universe? Nat was making wild guesses, scared of what she was thinking might be true.

"Of *your* world." Simon nodded.

"Like aliens?" Nat's voice came out in a rasp. She was having problems breathing, getting air in and out of her lungs. She was starting to feel light-headed.

"Like life and death..." Mitch clarified. "You're alive and we're—"

"Dead? You're ghosts?" Nat thought she might be close to passing out but with a rush of adrenaline, she shot to her feet and ran to the kitchen.

———

"OH, YOU DID that so well." Simon's sarcastic praise washed over Mitch without a sliver of guilt. "I'm so glad we did things your way."

"Give her a minute, will you? It's never easy to tell anyone and no one ever takes it well." Mitch stabbed his index finger in Simon's direction. "*That's* what all my years of experience has taught me."

"Are we going in after her?"

"You do what you want." With a dismissive wave, Mitch stalked across the room in the opposite direction Natalie had gone.

"I see. That's what you do, isn't it?" The tone in Simon's voice was meant to shame Mitch. "When things don't go the way you want, you walk away?"

Mitch wouldn't give Simon the satisfaction of a response. He kept his cool and his mouth shut.

"Maybe that's why you're still around. Have you ever thought of that? Maybe you need to learn to face your fears, Mister!"

Mitch bit his tongue to keep quiet and Simon headed for the kitchen.

Natalie stood at the sink and didn't look at Simon. He'd hoped she wasn't there to throw up. The news was upsetting, no doubt about that. If he could just say some magic words that would make acceptance... acceptance of him, and Mitch, easier, he'd do it.

"How you doing, hon?" he asked tentatively.

"Is it something I did?" The quiver in her voice said that she was near tears. "Was it bad? Must have been horrible to deserve this."

"No, oh, no. It's nothing like that." Simon wished he could rub her shoulders, do something to comfort her. "It's sort of a *fate* thing, out of our hands, nothing we can control, you know."

"So what does this mean? Are you haunting me?" She used a wadded-up paper towel to blot her nose.

"It's nothing like that. We're not evil spirits—although I can't vouch for the other one—" he jabbed his thumb over his shoulder, indicating Mitch— "But I can tell you that we're here for a good reason."

Tempted by what she heard, Natalie turned her head, peeking over her shoulder at Simon.

"I can't say what it is but there's always a good reason for it."

"For you or me?" She sniffed. "It's because I did something wrong, isn't it?" Simon looked so solid, so real. Natalie could almost believe he was a normal human being. But she'd seen him do things. Things that people didn't do. Unnatural thing... like pass through solid objects.

"For me, certainly. You... I don't know." Simon had his reasons for wanting Natalie's cooperation. "I can tell you for sure that we're not here to harm you in any way."

"How long will this last?"

"Until we figure out why we're here. What we're supposed to do. When we do it then we move on." He stared at her wide-eyed while she took it all in.

A few seconds of silence went by. Then a few more.

Simon tapped his wrist where a wristwatch would sit. "Aren't you supposed to be somewhere?"

Natalie glanced at the clock on the oven. "I'm going to be late." She dashed out of the kitchen with Simon hot on her heels.

———

RUNNING INTO HER bedroom and, subsequently, into her closet, Nat emerged with several garments on hangers. "How did you know I was supposed to be someplace?" She was growing more concerned about what he knew about her than who he was.

"I saw you with your sister this morning. You were telling her about your follow-up lunch with the restaurant's owner." Simon spoke to Nat, but his attention was clearly on the clothes lying on her bed.

"You *saw* Becca?" She stopped fussing with her wardrobe. So Nat wasn't imagining things. She had caught sight of Simon and Mitch earlier.

"*Saw* isn't exactly the right word. *Perceived* might be better." He narrowed his eyes, weighing the difference. "It's just a general feeling... a fuzzy someone, a presence, you know." Simon reclined on Nat's bed and made himself at home. "I don't *see* her in the same way I *see* you. But I know she's there. I know she had shoulder-length blonde hair and she was wearing a cute little flowered top."

"And how do you know all this about me, anyway? Can you read my mind?" Nat stopped and swiveled toward him. She tried to think of all the things she had thought, worried that he knew all about the awful things that must have been running through her head about how she was cracking up, about him, about Mitch, and who knew what else?

"No, I *cannot* read your mind." Simon blew out a puff of air in exasperation. "I'm dead, not deaf. I can hear things, conversations."

Nat had laid her clothes out on the bed next to him.

"Oh, my God—not wire hangers!" he shrieked, covering his mouth in shock.

If he'd been able to, Nat thought Simon would have yanked the hangers away and thrown them across the room. It's a good thing he could not touch her physical world.

She held up a sharp-looking and smart black jacket and a pair of matching pants.

"You're *not* wearing that, are you?" Simon eyed her with a sour expression.

"What's wrong with it?"

"It's the same outfit you wore yesterday—white shirt, black jacket, and black slacks."

"But they're not the same thing."

"But they still look exactly the same," Simon reiterated.

"Who made you the Fashion Police?" Someone wearing platform shoes wasn't one to give advice.

"Look—when I had my show everyone was always ready to *tune in and tone up with Simon!*" Simon flashed a 100 megawatt smile and struck a pose, not unlike that of John Travolta in Saturday Night Fever.

Nat had to stop and stare at his overly dramatic, ridiculous posture. "What is that?"

"My nationwide television show Simon Says, airing from the spring of 1982 to the winter of 1983. I was the hit of the daytime airwaves."

"What happened after 1983?" It was before her time. Nat was more than interested, but she was almost afraid to know the answer.

"That's when I started getting sick and it all ended." Simon grew quiet and added in a thoughtful whisper. "Had to sign off forever."

"Oh, sorry." Nat noticed his gleefulness ebb. Apparently, things hadn't ended well.

"Well, it happens to everyone." He shrugged and pointed at Nat's clothes. "But the point is that you wore exactly the same looking outfit yesterday to your interview and now you want to wear the identical thing for the lunch? This occasion is much more social, don't you think? Shouldn't you wear something softer and casual?"

"How do you know about my interview?" Nat turned her attention away from the clothes and stared at him.

"That's the first time I saw you." He twisted an imaginary little something between his fingers. "We weren't sure if you were one of us or not."

Nat narrowed her eyes. One of them. How was she ever going to get used to this?

"You'll get used to having us around. Dealing with people only you can see and others can't."

He *was* reading her mind.

"No, I can't read your mind. It's just written all over your face." He rolled his eyes. "Get over it. Let's move on." He gestured in a forward direction. "We need to get you ready for your big day. You need some flattering color by your face and for heaven's sake step out of those man-trousers, show some leg, woman."

Nat shrugged. She sensed that this was one battle she wasn't going to win. And maybe, just maybe, he had a point. If she was going to bother to show up she might as well put her well-shod foot forward. Which meant only one thing. It was time to raid Becca's closet.

3

NAT PULLED INTO the parking lot of Side Street Sam's South Bay sister restaurant Caldonia and stepped out of the car.

Mitch shouted out to her, "Hey, look at you, *doll*, you've got legs!"

The compliment made her blush. Not that she cared that he'd noticed but that he'd noticed at all.

"We were wondering when you'd show up." Simon unwrapped his scarf from his neck.

"No, we weren't." Mitch's hat sat on the hood of her car alongside his jacket and he worked on ridding himself of his tie, while all the while keeping his eyes on her.

Nat slid a peek at the two men flanking her and suppressed a smile.

"Give your skirt a little brush, would you?" Simon pointed at something that Nat wasn't sure existed. "There's a piece of fuzz, just there."

"Let me get that." Mitch smiled and leaned in to help. Of course, he couldn't.

Nat swiped her hand over the upper part of her right thigh, knowing there wasn't a thing Mitch could do about any fuzz.

"I gotta tell you that I like the skirt." The twinkle in Mitch's eyes told her how unmistakably pleased he was. There was no pretending there.

Nat couldn't imagine anyone getting excited over what she was wearing. She showed some leg but only up to her knee. Even though the pastel apricot shirt opened at the neck, it wasn't showing the slightest bit of cleavage, there was no enticing anything.

"It's not the clothes, doll, it's what's under them." Mitch winked. She could see his lips moving as he murmured something while his smoldering, dark gaze eased around her ankle and crept up the curve of her calf, moving higher and....

Nat ran her hand down her skirt, making sure he wasn't seeing anything she didn't want to expose. She swallowed. She had never felt so naked when fully dressed.

Mitch had movie star, roguish good looks with that cleft in his chin, he was devilishly handsome and then there was that mysterious expression. It was like he had some private X-rated fantasy going on inside his head. His charismatic presence was enough to derail any sane woman. What had he been like when he was alive?

"Could you just behave?" It would be Nat's last request. She didn't want anyone seeing her talk to no-one. "I'm trying to act normal, here. I don't want any of the other people to think I'm nuts."

"Other people?" Simon turned in a full circle to look around. "They can't see us." He stuck his thumbs in his ears and made an ugly face, and wiggled his fingers while sticking out his tongue. "See?"

"Don't make an ass out of yourself," Mitch scolded Simon. "Pardon my French." He nodded at Nat, apologizing.

Nat stopped in front of the hostess and said, "I'm here to meet with Nicholas Lockwood."

"Oh, the others are already seated. This way, please." The hostess motioned for Nat to follow her to the table.

All Nat had to do was relax and not react, pretend nothing was happening, no one else was talking. There wasn't a thing she could do about the two undead men but there was no way they could interfere with those around them, either. She had to remember that.

"Glad you could make it, Ms. Powell." Lockwood welcomed Nat and gestured for her to take a seat. "Now that you're all here I think you should get yourselves something to drink, have some lunch, and get to know each other. After you've had your meal we'll talk. How's that sound?"

The three potential employees agreed. Nat hadn't counted Simon or Mitch's votes.

Nicholas Lockwood had a friendly smile and he didn't seem like a stuffy businessman. It seemed to Nat that he genuinely cared about his staff, or potential staff, the surrounding patrons and their dining experience.

"I'll see you in a bit, then," Mr. Lockwood said after taking their drinks order and stepped away from the table, back toward the kitchen, "Enjoy your meal."

The three around the table eyed one another, a little shy and a bit cautious and of course they knew why the other two were there. They were all competing for the same job.

"I guess I'll go first," the pretty blonde spoke up. "I'm Janice Rhodes, I work at—"

"Well, hello there, Miss Janice." Mitch squeezed in between Janice and Nat, pulling up a non-existent chair. "Nice to make your acquaintance and under different circumstances, I would look forward to getting to know you better but Miss Natalie came along first." Mitch talked over Janice without her noticing but he'd prevented Nat from hearing what was said.

"I'm Paul Kwan, I'm assistant grill chef at—"

"Oh, a man who loves meat," Simon gushed over the handsome Asian man, working his way between Nat and Paul. "I'll just squeeze in right here. Oh, isn't this cozy?"

Wherever Paul had worked and what else he'd said had been lost with Simon's babbling.

Janice and Paul both stared at Nat, and in the growing silence, she figured it must have been her turn for an introduction.

"Oh, sorry. I'm Natalie Powell. I'm currently a line chef at 3rd Street Bistro." She smiled, wondering and waiting—maybe she should say something more.

Janice picked up her menu and Paul followed suit. Nat guessed she had said enough and followed their lead.

"What looks good?" Paul opened his menu. "I've heard a lot about them. All good, of course."

Janice laughed, taking a look at the lunch entrees. She probably thought the same thing they all thought. "Isn't that why we want to work for Mr. Lockwood at Sam's?"

"Doesn't that linguini with prosciutto and tomato cream sauce sound good?"

"Can't. I'm watching my carbs." Janice made a quick decision and closed the menu, setting it on the table in front of her. "I'm having the Seared Black Bass."

"Carbs?" Simon frowned and looked over to Nat clearly puzzled. "What's that?"

"I'm thinking the Wild Mushroom Risotto sounds pretty good." Paul was still buried behind the menu, deciding. "Or the Slow Braised Lamb."

"I was thinking about having the lamb, too." Nat mused. It was so difficult to make a decision. Just the thought of the dish made her mouth water.

"You can't have that. It's terrible for you, all fatty, and swimming in oil." Simon gestured wildly, demonstrating his outrage.

"Hey, butt out nosey Nellie," Mitch scolded. "Let the dame have what she wants."

"She might as well just stick it right on her hips." Simon stood, demonstrated by taking an imaginary shank in each hand, slapping it on the outside of each thigh, and took a few steps away from the table.

Nat sighed. Was her life reduced to listening to these two bozos argue over what was good for her and what wasn't?

"Have a salad—shrimp, crab, chicken," Simon suggested, pointing at the item on Nat's menu. "It's so much better for you— healthy, low fat, and low cal."

Nat was not going to cave to Simon's calorie tantrum.

"And don't forget" —Simon reminded her— "ask for the dressing on the side. That way you can pour on half and save your-self some extra calories."

Nat was not going to give in. Nobody, not even dead, was going to tell her what she could or could not eat. Forget it. It was her meal, her thighs.

"Yeah, the braised lamb sounds like a winner to me." Nat closed her menu and set it down in front of her. She'll show him who was calling the shots.

Simon turned away from Nat, crossing his arms in disgust.

"Good for you, *Toots*." Mitch smiled, slid closer to Nat, resting his arm on the back of her seat. Nat leaned ever-so-slightly away. Even though he couldn't touch her, he was still getting a little too close for comfort.

"Hello, I'm Joshua and I'll be your server this afternoon." A tall, good looking, blond young man in a neat white shirt, tie, and a white apron over his black slacks held a pad next to their table. "Are you ready to order?"

"Go ahead," Nat urged Janice to go first.

"I'll have the Seared Bass and Pellegrino with a lemon twist." Janice handed her menu to Joshua.

"And you, Miss?" Joshua turned to Nat.

"Think of your thighs," Simon pleaded in a desperate whisper.

Nat knew what she wanted and what she should have. "Can I go last?" Nat didn't want to order under pressure.

"All right." Joshua turned to Paul. "Sir?"

"The Mushroom Risotto and Perrier."

"With lemon or lime twist?"

"No, just plain. Thanks."

"Very well." Joshua glanced at Nat and must have sensed her indecision. "Mr. Lockwood has plans to join you for dessert and has preordered a chocolate soufflé."

"Dessert?" Simon collapsed into his chair with the shock of it all. "Disaster."

"Relax, Calorie King." Mitch must have gotten tired of Simon's dramatics and decided to finally pipe up and say something.

"Just because you like your women Rubenesque doesn't mean you should encourage Natalie to plump up." Simon snapped back at Mitch.

"A woman's not a real woman unless she's got some dangerous curves to navigate." Mitch defended his opinion, leaning forward he urged Nat, "You go right on ahead, *doll*, have your lamb."

There was something in the way Mitch said it that bugged her. The way he kept eyeing her like she was the next course on his plate.

Well, no thank you.

"I've changed my mind. I'll have the orange chicken salad with a glass of ice tea." Nat closed her menu and held it out.

Joshua jotted down her order and collected all the menus, Nat's first.

"Oh, and, Joshua, could I have the dressing on the side, please?"

It wasn't that Nat was listening to Simon as much as she didn't want, in any way, to please Mitch.

―――――――

"THIS IS FAIRLY awkward," Paul said after they all had ordered. "They leave three candidates for the same job sitting together. Can we talk about this or is it weird?" He glanced from Nat to Janice, pushed his utensils to the edge of his placemat, and dove in. "I never thought I'd hear from *Sam's*. It's been nearly three weeks since I interviewed."

"Just over a week for me," Janice added. "I thought they got back to me pretty quick."

"I interviewed with them just yesterday." Nat shrugged. "I thought it was kind of amazing I got a call so soon."

"Lunch... with Mr. Lockwood. Who would have thought?" Janice took a sip of water.

"He owns three or is it four restaurants in the Bay Area?" Paul scanned the room, checking out the details of the dining room.

"Thank goodness Daine Owens can only be in one place at a time."

Daine Owens. Nat hated to hear his name.

"I thought Owens had crossed me off the list for sure." Paul sounded as defeated as Nat had felt that day when she'd faced her old colleague.

"I don't think he likes anyone." Janice didn't find it surprising that no one liked him.

"I've heard that he's never satisfied with anyone's performance, he's a complete perfectionist." Paul shook his head. "But that doesn't mean I'm giving up this job.

Neither was Janice from the look on her face.

Joshua appeared at the table with a tray. A small plate appeared before Simon and he scooted toward the table as if Joshua had brought something just for him.

"Mr. Lockwood sends these with his compliments." Joshua set a plate with four different types of appetizers right in front of Simon.

"Oh, look, cheese puffs, my favorite." He pulled an *hors d'oeuvre* from the plate in front of him.

"Nothing for me, thanks." Mitch let out his breath and smiled. "I'll just feast my eyes on the delights of Miss Natalie, here."

"Could you give the lame pick-up lines a rest?" Simon reached out for a cheese puff, but his hand passed through the small puffed pastry.

"Just because you don't care for the ladies or, should I say, the ladies don't care for you."

"What are you talking about?" Simon screeched. "The ladies *love* me. You're just jealous. At least I had my 15 minutes of fame, unlike you, you Silver Screen wanna-be. The King of Hollywood tried to make you his heir but the public was too smart, they wouldn't have any of it."

"Put a cork in it, would you?" Mitch's voice grew louder. "You've always got something to say, don't you, loudmouth? Always have to have that last word."

"Would you two just shut up?" Nat's eyes flew open when she realized she'd said that out loud. Janice and Paul froze and locked their gazes to Nat.

"I'm sorry—" Nat said, knowing that no matter what she said it would never excuse or explain her irrational outburst. "I didn't mean that."

Simon didn't seem to take any notice that Nat had said anything at all. "What's the matter, Tough Guy?" He continued to taunt Mitch. "Can't stand up to the truth?"

Mitch stood, his eyes smoldering with contained rage. He

looked like he was ready to punch Simon. Instead, Simon disappeared. Right in front of Nat's eyes.

Mitch let out a disappointed sigh. Almost as if he were sorry, his sparring partner had left. "Would it be terrible of me to leave you alone?" Mitch at least had the decency to ask. "You think you can handle it, *doll*?"

Nat flashed the smallest of smiles and a slow but distinct nod. Mitch faded away.

Alone. At last. It was a miracle. Nat might have made a fool of herself in front of Janice and Paul. As long as the gruesome twosome kept clear and she could keep her mind on her job interview when Mr. Lockwood was here, she might have a fair chance at getting this job.

———

NAT PARKED BECCA'S car safe and sound, in one whole, unblemished, complete working order piece in the employee section of the Barnes & Noble parking lot with the sunshade firmly placed in the front windshield. She handed the key fob to her sister all before 2 p.m. If she wanted to continue borrowing the car, Nat would jump through the car parking hoops, doing whatever Becca wanted to ensure there would be a next time.

After that afternoon's wonderful follow-up lunch at Caldonia, Nat was in for another long day. She still had some time before she had to show up for work. Not enough to go home, but time enough, she decided, for a quick stop at her café for a much-needed sit-down and some coffee.

Heading for the front of the Barnes & Noble, Nat felt completely exhausted. Maybe she needed a double shot of espresso to keep her going. Maybe she'd been pushing herself too hard. Maybe the ghost-thing had been all made up.

She stopped. Right in front of the TV & Movie books section.

Was that a sign or what? Nat scanned the five shelves of books, two sections wide and wondered.

Hmm.

Were those two guys she'd seen real? Had her sleep-deprived brain made up the whole thing? This was her chance to check. Were they real or not?

She glanced around, looking not for anyone watching her, but for her supposed-spooks Simon and Mitch. Bumping into them now might prove embarrassing because she was checking up on their stories.

Nat stepped closer to the front of the Television section. Skimming the titles on the spines: TV Classics—The Early Years, Encyclopedia of TV and History of Television. She stopped at TV 1980s.

Opening the book to the Table of Contents, she then flipped to the index, looking for Simon Says. Page 87, it was listed under the section called More Than Just Personality. On the upper left-hand corner, Nat recognized a picture of Simon in the same scary John Travolta pose that she'd seen before. There he stood with several women behind him dressed in multi-colored leotards, coordinating headbands, knee-high legwarmers, and very big hair. The caption read:

Simon Dijon: His was a trendy way to shape up to the Top 40 hits of the day. His distinctive personality along with his savvy advice on diet, personal style, and healthy living made this show popular.

Shades of Richard Simmons. The book fell closed in Nat's hands and she pushed it back into place. Looking off to the side, she spotted a section of books dedicated to wartime films. Hollywood's World War II seemed to leap out at her. She pulled it out from the bottom shelf and hefted the book, it weighed a ton.

She paged through the index for... the other guy. Mitch. What was his name? She glanced away from the book, out the window and blinked at the sunlight, concentrating on Mitch's full name.

Mitchell? Oh, yes. She remembered. Mitchell Hudson.

Hudson, Mitchell page 156.

Combat America - 1943
351st Bombardment Group of the U.S. Army Air Forces' documentary based in England during the Second World War. The air and ground crews are followed through bombing missions over Hitler's Germany.

Starring: Clark Gable, William Hatcher, Philip Hulls, Mitchell Hudson, Daniel Stevens, Paul Posti, Henry Arnold.

Under the brief paragraph, a black and white photo of the men wearing leather bomber jackets stood in front of a plane. Nat squinted at the faces, trying to recognize someone other than Clark Gable. Maybe the third man in from the left in the last row?

Nat couldn't be certain that it was him. But it looked like him.

So that meant they were real, both of them. Alive. Once. A long time ago.

———

NAT SOMEHOW MANAGED to get to the Sky Blue Café in her daze. A quad-espresso wouldn't have been strong enough to bring her around to the normal world.

She just sat there, staring at her ornately decorated demitasse cup. She really did see dead people. However, she hadn't seen them lately and it had been at least three hours. Nat had better just enjoy being alone while it lasted.

She gathered the sections of the local Chronicle newspaper: want ads, real estate, sports, entertainment, local, and finally, the front page. The front-page story with a picture read: *Local Heiress Discovered Dead*. Nat pushed the newspaper to one side and lifted her scone off its plate, raising it to her mouth.

"I swear if you take a bite into that I'll— I'll—" Simon paused with his mouth open ready to finish his threat.

"There isn't a damn thing you can do." Mitch scolded Simon who appeared in a chair across from her. He pulled his hat off his head and held it to his chest. "Pardon my French, Miss Natalie."

"This isn't about my thighs again, is it?" Nat glanced at Simon without moving the scone even a millimeter away from her lips.

"I hate that hat." Mitch dropped it onto the stacked newspapers.

"Not your thighs, that'll go right to your tummy," Snooty Simon preached, doing his best to convince Nat to desert her afternoon pastry. "Did you have that chocolate soufflé at lunch?"

Nat didn't answer but Simon seemed to know that she had. She hoped she hadn't looked as guilty as she felt.

"With whipped cream?"

"There was a little on the side." She barely touched any of it.

"Well, Missy, if you keep eating like this that little jelly-belly wiggle around your midsection will turn into a solid jelly roll before long."

"I really like jelly rolls," she stated longingly. A man walked by and shot her a glance, clearly thinking she was weird because she was talking to herself. Or to the currant scone she held to her lips.

Nat set the scone on its plate. She opened her purse, dug out her cell phone.

"Why are you holding a compact to your ear?" Simon motioned to the side of his own head, mimicking her.

"It's not a compact. It's a cell phone," Nat said as if she were speaking normally. "So people don't think I'm sitting here talking to myself."

"A woman's make-up compact is a telephone?" Mitch stared at Nat, puzzled.

"Does Cover Girl do cordless phones now?" Simon said in a way that Nat couldn't tell if he was confused or just being sarcastic.

"A cell phone is—" Nat was going to explain. "Oh, forget it." She moved the phone to her other ear. It would just take too long. "So, my cell phone and my scone aside, what are you guys doing here now?"

"I'm here because I hadn't seen you since lunch and I've missed you." Mitch flashed a smile at Nat. "Meeting you has made me wish I were alive again."

Who was he kidding?

"Does that line work on anyone?" Simon rolled his eyes. "Totally lame."

"What?" Mitch shrugged and glanced from Nat to Simon. "I'm being honest, here."

Simon glanced skyward and exhaled. "Can we get serious?" He waited for a few seconds before starting. "We've talked about it and come to a decision."

And Nat waited.

"Our mission, the reason the two of us" —Simon indicated Mitch and himself— "have been sent here, to you, and why you can see us. Whatever it is, involves the three of us. We're supposed to all do it together."

AFTER 3rd STREET Bistro had closed for the evening, Nat strolled out to the same booth she'd seen Simon and Mitch at the night before.

Simon sat with a martini glass in hand as if he were enjoying himself at his favorite watering hole. Mitch sat slumped against the wall with his legs stretched out on the bench. He sat up when he saw Nat coming his way.

"You guys look like you're working hard." Nat had finished for the night and was on her way out.

"You get used to waiting when you've been doing it for as long as I have." Mitch slid to his right, making room for Nat to sit next to him.

"Patience is a virtue. Remember that." Simon winked and raised his glass.

"How long does this go on?" Life would return to normal, wouldn't it? Nat hoped. Some day. Someday soon? "When will we know? Do we get some kind of message?"

"What? Are you in a hurry?" Simon looked as if Nat had said something rude.

"Don't tell me that you want to get rid of us. Just when I'm thinking that I couldn't go on without you." Mitch pressed his hand to his heart.

"Well, *normal* people don't go around life with a gruesome twosome tailing them, even in the twenty-first century." Nat glanced skyward. "I'd say that most people don't even have one ghost following them."

"Look, *doll*, we were once *normal* people, too," Mitch said, perhaps harsher than he meant.

That's what Nat had figured out that afternoon. She was still trying to come to terms with it.

A shimmer of light drew Nat's attention to the right. By the time she'd turned her head, she had to squint against the light. It had intensified to a sudden blinding flash before disappearing.

"What's that?" Simon leaned out of the booth and around Nat to see.

A young blonde woman sat alone at a table.

"Do you see her?" Simon whispered.

Mitch leaned out of the booth to sneak a peek. "Yup."

"I do, too," Nat added. That woman had not been there before. As crazy as it sounded, Nat could have sworn the flash of light had brought her.

No one said anything for the next few minutes. They all remained still and stared where they'd seen the flash of light—from one another to the woman and back again.

"What do you think?" Simon whispered cautiously, breaking the silence. "Is she one of us or one of you?"

It was difficult to get a good look at her with her head down, resting on her folded arms on the table in front of her. But she soon lifted her head and Nat glimpsed the woman's pretty face when she swiped her cheek with her hand.

"She's on your side," Nat said, absolutely positive and gulped.

"How can you be so sure?" Did Simon ever take anyone at their word?

Nat's mouth went dry, she could hardly get the words out. "Because I saw the story of her murder on the front page of today's paper."

4

NAT HAD HEARD about her death on the radio, seen the young woman's picture on the television, even read the headlines in the newspaper.

"Her name is Georgette Price. She was found dead in her home this morning," Nat reported to her companions just as the news anchor had.

"Georgette, huh? Well, then she's only just arrived." Simon sounded as if she'd flown in from LA and not made the big journey to *The Other Side*.

"It's going to be a while before she's able to talk to us." Mitch didn't sound very hopeful and settled back in his seat in dismay or defeat.

"A while? How long is a while?" In *eternity* terms it could be a very long time.

"First there's the readjustment" —Simon ticked off on his index finger— "There's always some undefined amount of time one goes through while in the— the... what shall we call it... the... waiting room while you figure out what happened and where you are."

"Waiting room?" Nat echoed confused. Now Simon made it sound as if he were talking about a doctor's office.

"And it was shoulder to shoulder when I got there. Don't get me started about the line to get out." He ticked off his middle finger. "Then you see your beloved friends and family." He turned to Nat. "That part is so fun, it makes you feel wonderful. If it weren't for the fact that you realized that you're seeing people who've died which means you're dead... well, it's not as much of a shock as you think. You kind of get used to the idea that something's happened to you."

Nat squeezed her eyes closed and tried to follow his line of thinking.

"I didn't have much of a crowd waiting for me when I got there," Mitch said casually.

"Big surprise." Simon gasped in mock-shock.

"Not even your parents?" Nat thought that would be most likely the people to show up.

"They were still alive when I died."

"Brothers? Sisters? Friends?"

"No siblings. Just my buddies from the war." Mitch's eyes glazed over. "I didn't expect to see them."

The conversation was getting creepy. Nat didn't want to hear anymore.

"Well, if Georgette is already here" —Simon brought them back on topic— "Then that means that she has to be—" He stopped. "Only this morning, you say?" He looked puzzled. "That can't be right. It's too quick."

"Don't look at me." Nat shrugged. "I'm just reporting the facts as I hear them."

"Well, there's one way to find out for sure." Mitch made to slide across the bench and leave.

"Don't go over there now." Simon grabbed Mitch's sleeve,

stopping him. "She won't be ready yet. You don't want to give her a fright."

"It's not as if I can scare her to death," Mitch said. Simon's hold on him kept him from moving.

"No, you don't." Simon let Mitch go and waved him back. "Trust me, it's really better that we wait for a while. It took weeks before I figured out what was going on and that was after I'd seen my Dearly Departed."

"Weeks?" Nat couldn't imagine waiting around for that long. She wanted her life to get back to normal.

"I think I must have been out of it for at least a month." Mitch chimed in.

"A month?" Nat mouthed, incredulous at how much time this could take. "Is that how long we'll have to wait until she talks to us?"

Simon studied Georgette, his expression was one of concern. "The poor dear is going to need some TLC. All right, maybe there is something we can do to help her along."

Simon and Mitch slid out of their booth. Simon's attention focused on Georgette before heading slowly her way.

Mitch leaned toward Nat. "You find out what you can about her and we'll do our best to settle her in and open up." He stared at her, looking as if he were trying to memorize her face. "I'm gonna miss seeing you, *doll*." He winked and walked over to Simon and Georgette. Then all three of them vanished.

OVER THE NEXT several days, Nat collected any and all the information she could about Georgette Price which pretty much amounted to several news stories besides her obituary.

Georgette had been a young heiress who'd come into her father's fortune when he passed away six months earlier at the age of 87. It seemed Georgette was more of a young socialite, spending most of her time with wealthy friends in Aspen or Cannes, flying to London or Paris for a designer's new fashion line, or dashing off for an exotic vacation in the Mediterranean or a remote island in the South Seas.

None of the articles mentioned who was running her father's business, managing her money, or who might be inheriting the Price fortune following her death. The police still had not released any additional details, it was referred to as an ongoing investigation.

It had been almost a week and Nat hadn't seen a sign of the ghostly trio. Again, she questioned her sanity and wondered if her new companions weren't something she'd made up. What she did get was several nights of solid rest. She could almost get used to this.

Surfacing from a wonderful night's sleep, Nat felt the cotton pillowcase soft against her face. She lay in bed with her eyes closed and took a deep breath. The sheet pulled up to her chin, still had a freshly laundered smell.

Easing her eyelids open, she saw a man next to her in bed and let out a bloodcurdling scream. Loud enough to jolt her wide awake. Loud enough to wake the neighbors on all sides of her apartment. Loud enough to wake the dead.

Her bedroom door burst open. "What? What's the matter?" Barely wrapped in her robe, Becca stared at Nat.

Only Nat. Because Nat knew that Becca couldn't see Mitch tucked in beside her with only a smug smile and a heavy growth of morning stubble that couldn't come close to masking the deep cleft in his chin. What she did see was Nat clutching her top bed sheet to her chest.

"Nothing," Nat said in an artificially calm voice. She was doing her best to look through Mitch and at her sister. "I had a bad dream, sorry." He was not an easy sight to ignore.

"Jeez, you scared the pee out of me." Relief swept over Becca's face. "I thought you were being murdered or something." She exhaled and backed out of the room , pulling the door closed behind her.

"Yeah, *or something*." Nat groaned, still trying to catch her breath.

"Give you a little start, did I?" Mitch quipped in a first-thing-in-the-morning growl.

He could not have slept there all night next to her. Nat glared at him. Ghosts didn't sleep, did they?

There was a knock at her door before it swung open. "Oh, Nat." Becca poked her head in.

Nat peered up wide-eyed at her sister.

Becca glanced around, doing a quick check. Had Nat looked as guilty as she felt? Had she suspected someone was with Nat? "I'm going to be spending a few nights at Theo's." She pointed, presumably, at him. "I just wanted to let you know what was going on."

"With Theo. Got it." Nat smiled, nodding her head. She hadn't a clue they'd gotten so close already.

"And I left the car fob in its dish by the phone in the kitchen just in case you need the car." Becca leaned back, shutting the door behind her.

"Thanks, Beck," Nat said through the door.

Muffled voices and rustling from outside Nat's bedroom grew softer. Nat glared at Mitch, waiting until she heard Becca's bedroom door close.

"What do you think you're doing?" She made sure not to raise her voice. Mitch could talk as loud as he wanted, no one heard him except her.

"Just thought I'd take advantage of the local scenery." He pried his eye open to peek at her.

She didn't like the way he was looking at her. With both eyes open it was nearly obscene like she hadn't been wearing a stitch of clothing.

"I bet your skin is soft. I wish I could touch you. All those luscious hills and valleys of your—"

"You need to keep quiet." Nat could feel his gaze skimming the outline of her hips up to her arm to her breasts. She pressed the sheet harder to her chest but it didn't seem as if a mere 300 thread count could keep him from seeing her.

"It's not my moaning she's complaining about. I've never been a heavy breather."

Nat was not moaning or breathing heavy.

"What's the big deal, anyway? It's not like I'm in any condition to do anything about it, right?" He pushed the covers down to his waist.

It didn't matter if he could or not, and that wasn't the point. "I don't know if I feel safe around a guy like you. No matter what *condition* you're in."

"Oh, come on, lighten up." He raised his hands above his head and stretched with a groan. "You could do a lot worse than a guy like me."

"Get out of my bed." She watched him push up to a sitting position and stared at his very well-toned naked back with his muscles bunching and lengthening. He had some nerve talking to her like that. "Where are your clothes?"

"That's a fairly personal question." He looked over his shoulder and smiled. "I don't know if we know one another well enough to be talking about states of undress."

"You're the naked one in *my* bed." She pointed out as if he didn't know. "*I* have clothes on."

As he moved to stand, the sheet fell away from his back and Nat averted her eyes in a moment of modesty, thinking she shouldn't look, but his tush was fully visible he vanished.

PLANTED ON THE living room sofa, Simon swung his crossed leg with impatience when Nat stepped out of her bedroom. "Are you two finished playing footsie in there?"

"I did nothing to encourage him." Nat skirted right by Simon and headed to the kitchen for some coffee and whatever breakfast she could rustle up.

Simon cleared his throat and held up his hand. "Oh, no. I am not my brother's keeper. But then again, Mitch is not my brother."

"I'm certainly not going to blame you for what he does." She filled the coffee mug that she'd pulled from the cabinet. Had Simon done something so wrong in life that he had to put up with Mitch now? Was this some sort of cosmic justice? Nat had no idea how the *other side* worked.

"No manners at all. He's such a tramp." Simon shook his head. "A bad, very bad boy." He moved toward the counter where Nat stood. "I honestly don't think he knows how to behave any other way."

"Simon?" Nat kept her voice soft and low. While Becca and her boyfriend had left, the neighbors were still around. "Is there a reason you're here?"

"Oh, yes!" His face brightened as he gasped with animated surprise. "She's here. Georgie. She's ready to see you."

Georgette Victoria Price. In person.

Nat felt like she was about to meet some kind of superstar. Here was a woman she'd read about for the last week, every article she could Google, listened to any local or national news stories and now she would come face to face, sort of, with her.

"All I ask is that you be careful. She's still fragile." Simon warned, moving away toward the floral overstuffed chair. "I don't think she was this way when she was alive. I'm sure it's just PDT."

P-D-T?

"Post-*death* trauma," he explained after reading what must have been Nat's puzzled expression.

Of course.

"Come on, dear. This way." Simon spoke skyward and gestured toward the chair, which Nat thought must be the place where Simon wanted Georgette to appear. "Natalie, here, wants to meet you."

The once young, vibrant, fashionable, and vivacious Georgette Price materialized in the chair with a glistening silver sparkle that vanished. She appeared quiet, meek, and nothing like what Nat had imagined about the young woman who was once so full of life.

Georgette sat straight-backed, her legs crossed at the ankles. Dressed in a soft pink long-sleeved, scoop-necked sweater, and a skirt, she looked more fashion magazine-worthy than Nat had alive.

"I'm *still* wearing the same thing. *Si*-mon!" Georgette let out a strangled gasp and stared down, gesturing at her clothes.

"I told you that it'll be a while." Simon patted her hand. "And you won't be spending eternity in that outfit."

"I'm only wearing this little gold necklace with this tiny fresh-water pearl and these crocodile pumps." Georgette uncrossed her ankles and extended her legs to show the pointy-toe shoes on her feet. "I don't even have a purse!"

That was more the Diva behavior Nat would have expected. And had the spoiled-rich-girl-who-had-always-gotten-what-she-wanted-and-couldn't-cope-with-anything-less act down to perfection.

"Don't worry, honey. It'll be fine. Georgie, I'd like you to meet someone." He did his best to focus her attention elsewhere. "This is Natalie." Simon stepped aside and swept his hand toward Nat. "This is Georgette Price, but she likes to be called Georgie."

"Hello, Georgie," Nat said in her calmest voice. She wasn't sure how to ease into a conversation, knowing that asking-how-she-was wouldn't be a good way to start.

"Are you dead, too?" Georgie's voice was on the high-pitched side and soft.

"Me? No, I'm— I haven't—" Nat stammered, shocked at her question.

"Natalie is still living." Simon clarified. "She's not on our side."

"Did I know you? Before I died, I mean." Georgie glanced from Simon to Nat.

"No. I didn't know you when you were aliv—" Nat stopped. That probably wasn't the right thing to say, either. "We've never met."

"You can talk about her" —Simon paused— "*death*, that's all right. She knows."

No matter what Simon said about Georgie, knowing her *condition*, Nat did not feel comfortable about it as a general topic.

"I didn't go on my own, I can tell you that. I had help getting here."

"Do you know who" —Nat tried to swallow the six-quart sauce pan-sized lump in her throat before saying the awful— "Killed you?"

"No, I don't. But I will," Georgie said with a faraway look in her eyes. "And when I do, that person will be sorry. I'm going to haunt them for the rest of their life."

Nat caught Simon exchanging looks with Mitch who stood just to Nat's right at the end of the kitchen counter.

Mitch? When had he popped in?

He'd discarded his jacket, hat, and tie and had unbuttoned his shirt to roll up his sleeves which meant he must have been there for a while.

Apparently, neither he nor Simon approved of Georgie's threat or maybe *revenge* was an afterlife-don't. They were, after all, supposed to be in a higher plane above all that kind of petty stuff?

"Simon thinks we're supposed to help her," Mitch told Nat, so only she could hear. "Figure out who snuffed her."

"We're supposed to find her murderer?" Nat felt her knees go weak, she moved from the kitchen and eased into the sofa. She was a chef, not a detective.

She cooked food, not solved crimes. However, Nat would admit that some people's cooking was a crime.

"What have you found out?" Simon prompted and waited, ever-alert, for Nat's answer.

Nat repeated the facts from the newspaper, the society pages, small articles she'd dug up online and ended with, "The funeral is today."

"Today?" Georgie stood as if she were about to take action or run to the closest upscale department store. "This cashmere sweater and pencil skirt are fine for a dinner party, for *one* evening, but I can't go to my funeral looking like this."

"Don't worry, that's when your clothes will change," Simon reassured her.

"Dinner party?" Mitch was the first to pounce on that tidbit of news which must have been new. "You never told us that you'd been to a dinner party that night. Where was it? Who was there?"

"Did I say that?" Georgie narrowed her eyes in concentration. "A dinner party? I don't know. I can't remember being at a party."

"Don't fret about it." Simon rubbed Georgie's shoulder and gave Mitch a hardened look. "It'll come to you. Just give it time."

"Not remembering is so frustrating." Georgie soaked up all the sympathy Simon offered.

"I know, I know." Simon patted her hand and gave her a shoulder to lean on.

"Can we go? Now?" Georgie stared from Simon to Nat to Mitch looking hopeful.

"Go? Where?" Nat felt as if she'd missed an entire chunk of conversation.

"Where are my services being held?"

"The Price mansion," Nat repeated from memory.

"At home." Georgie closed her eyes and a dreamy smile spread over her lips. "My home."

"I'm so glad," Simon commented. "Funeral parlors can be so tacky."

"I can't do anything about my clothes but you have got to change." Georgie stared at Nat like she was Raggedy Ann on her way to a Black Tie affair. "And don't you dare make me late for my own funeral."

5

AFTER REREADING GEORGIE'S obituary, Nat discovered she had just over two hours to get to the service. This set a fire under Georgie and her demands beginning with the 'Don't-make-me-late' comment was the first of many complaints Georgie had for Nat. Next was the 'You're-not-going-to-wear-that,' repeated a multitude of times about Nat's inadequate wardrobe.

Nat's ears were pretty full by the time she had made it to the car. When she got there, Georgie added, "You can't be serious. I'm not arriving at the house in that."

Simon's snide, "It's not like anyone will see you," was the murmured response before he rolled his eyes.

It occurred to Nat that a Volkswagen Bug must not have been Georgie's style. As it turned out, the *ghosties* did not care to travel by car. Nat did not need to put up with them for the ride to Hillsborough, a ritzy area south of San Francisco. She was more than glad to hear them say they'd see her there.

Nat parked the farthest away from the residence. The Bug stood out woefully among the Porches, Jags, and Beemers. As if on cue, Simon, Georgie, and Mitch appeared next to Nat when she stepped out of the car.

"Why couldn't you have your driver take you in the Bentley or the Escalade or even a limo?" Georgie complained for the fifteenth time.

"Because not everyone has a limo at their disposal." Simon was kind enough to answer for Nat. "Nat's like us, just plain folk."

Nat was glad Simon stood up for her. She figured that arguing with Georgie was a no-win situation. It was clear that Georgie had had everything she wanted. She wasn't as much spoiled as just plain rich and used to getting her own way.

"I really don't know what I'm doing here," Nat said in a whisper mostly to herself.

"You're here to help Georgie." Mitch reminded her. "We all are."

"She's going through a traumatic time," Simon added in a caring voice. "We've all got to be supportive."

Supportive for Nat meant attending the funeral because Georgie wanted to go. Supportive also meant wearing Becca's single strand of pearls, which according to Georgie, were low quality, over a pale pink shirt, which was Georgie's favorite color.

"Did you have to wear that?" Georgie grumbled at Mitch after giving Nat and Simon the once over.

"Don't blame me." Mitch bristled, pulling his hat off and tossing it away. "I didn't choose this."

"You know the saying, 'You can't take it with you?'" Simon said smartly. "Well, on this side we say, 'once you have it, you're stuck with it.' He's wearing the same suit and accessories, however undesirable they are, every time he reappears."

"Don't complain to me. I hate that hat." Mitch said *hat* as if it were a four letter word. "I dump the thing every chance I get." He tossed it away as they walked toward the house. "I don't know what wise guy decided I had to have that. If I ever find out, I'll—" He stopped, noticing that he was being stared at. "Never mind."

Simon motioned to his suit with a wave of his hand. "This double-breasted number is classic."

Nat glanced at him in his high turtleneck and worked hard not to roll her eyes. Who was he kidding? She was not about to break the news to him that he was just wrong.

"That scarf has seen better days." Mitch, who managed to look sharp even in his vintage-wear, had that old-world classic handsome. It's no wonder Clark Gable thought he might make it on the big screen.

Poor Simon looked like an old Disco dude, stepping right out of a Miami Vice rerun with his wide lapels and pleated slacks. Except in his day, the TV show probably wasn't in reruns, they were airing in Primetime.

"There's nothing wrong with my scarf." Simon glanced down at his clothes.

"Went out decades ago. Unless one's expecting a blizzard." Mitch sounded like someone who'd been paying attention to fashion trends as time had gone by.

"What about me?" Georgie turned to Simon. "This can't be happening. I'm still wearing the same thing. Even though pink is my favorite color, a pink cashmere sweater and a pencil skirt is not what I should be wearing to a funeral."

"Trust me," Simon said for the umpteenth time and threw a hard look at Mitch over his shoulder, warning him to back off. "You won't be wearing it for long."

"Oh, my gosh. Look at that." Georgie pointed toward the house.

The only thing Nat could see *was* the house. Mansion. It was enormous, one of the grand estate homes that covered the top of the rolling hill with landscaped yards on all sides. A circular sweeping drive led to the front of the house from the main road miles away.

"It's Skinner." Georgie sniffed, getting misty-eyed. "I can see him. I mean really, really *see* him."

So she was beginning to see things and people around her. Simon had already explained to Nat how they *perceived* her world. Georgie must have gotten to the point where she could recognize faces.

"He's the most wonderful butler." Georgie sighed as if she were staring at a long lost friend. It was the first bit of real warmth Nat had seen.

Simon, Mitch, and Nat all stared at Georgie, eyebrows raised. And Nat was pretty sure they were all thinking the same thing—a *butler*?

"Name please?" Skinner intoned when Nat reached the front door at the top of the steps.

"Ah—Natalie Powell." Nat only understood the significance of giving her name when he brought a small leather-bound notebook out from behind his back.

"It's so good to see him again," Georgie continued. "He is absolutely the best, so dependable. A rock."

"I'm sorry," Skinner said in a tone that was wholly unapologetic. "I don't seem to find your name on the guest list."

"Umm." A guest list. For a funeral. Nat felt a little awkward. Maybe she could turn around and go home. She wasn't all that excited about attending the funeral in the first place but had tried for Georgie's sake.

"Wait a minute." Georgie stopped and tilted her head. "I hear something else. People talking. Other people." She was having a hard time catching her breath and half-sobbed, holding back her emotions. "Not just any people... it's Liz and Dahlia. I can see them, too!"

Nat could hear them, now. Two young, blonde women passing through the foyer. One wore a mostly black dress with leopard trim and matching shoes; the other, a pink satin camisole and gray beaded cardigan.

"I'm going to miss Georgie so much," the one in the animal print said.

"Me, too." The one in the sweater replied. "Who's going to help me pick out my shoes?"

Simon glanced at her feet and feigned horror. "Obviously someone's got to help you. Those fake dead animals on your feet are ghastly."

"I told her to buy those months ago." Georgie's voice lost all traces of sadness and grew defensive. "They match her new satchel we picked up in London."

"Well, dear, you clearly had a lapse in judgment that day."

"What do you know, you're still dressing like it's still Disco days!" Georgie leaned toward Simon ready to bite his ear off.

"Listen here, Betsy-bottle-blonde—" Simon turned at her ready to launch a counterattack.

"Knock it off, you two." Mitch inserted himself between them. "If this is going to be a fashion attack, then I'm out of here."

Simon waved an overenthusiastic goodbye and Mitch dissolved into nothingness.

"That's Liz in the pink, wearing her new Pradas and Dahlia carrying the Dooney & Bourke barrel tiger-print satchel." Georgie broke into a new bout of tears mingled in with her tears of joy. "They're my two closest and best friends in the whole wide world. I can't believe I'm seeing them again."

"You need to calm down. Just try and take it easy." Simon tried to comfort her.

"They're so sad that I'm gone." Georgie sniffed. "They look so beautiful. And I'm not with them."

"Liz! Dahlia!" Nat called past the butler to them in an impulsive move.

The two managed to put aside their personal grief and noticed

Nat waving at them. Skinner backed away as Liz and Dahlia approached the door with caution.

"I'd know you two anywhere, Georgie's told me so much about you both. You're her two closest and best friends in the whole wide world." Nat seasoned her voice to match Georgie's exuberant delivery. "I'm sure you don't know me. She may have never even mentioned me. We just met a few months before she— ah... passed."

"Right before Dahlia bought her Pradas on our stopover in New York on our way to Paris," Georgie recalled. "She couldn't decide between them or the Spaulding and Gublo silk and satin pumps. They weren't right for her, you know?"

No, Nat didn't.

"I told her that you couldn't go wrong with Prada."

"Do you know... I mean, you *knew* Georgie?" By the questioning tone in Liz's voice and the puzzled look on her face, Nat could tell she wasn't buying it.

Dahlia eyed Nat and didn't say a word. She seemed the tougher of the two to convince.

"You have to make them believe you, Natalie." Georgie urged. "Go on, you have to keep trying. Don't give up."

Nat knew she couldn't. "We weren't the best of friends but I know she'd want me to be here."

"I don't know." Dahlia readjusted the strap of her tiger print bag on her arm. Her chilly stare said it all. "You just don't seem the type that she'd be friends with."

Nat shrugged, acknowledging their skepticism. "I'm a chef. She came to me with questions about her dietary concerns. She wanted to eat *healthier.*"

"She was going to hire you? Replace Alberto?" Liz found the idea outrageous.

Dahlia turned to Liz. "Alberto's been here forever, he ran the kitchen for Georgie's father. She's been thinking about a new personal chef ever since her father died. She wanted someone more—"

"Pacific-Rim, California cuisine," Georgie said.

"Pacific-Rim, California cuisine," Nat repeated.

"*Pacific-Rim, California cuisine,*" Dahlia mimicked in apparent awe of Nat's dead-on perfect answer.

Nat flashed a friendly smile and continued, "As different as we were, we just ended up hitting it off." She checked Dahlia and Liz's expressions. Was she making any headway?

"And she told you things about us?" Dahlia shared Liz's wide-eyed stare of having their most secret secrets being revealed to this no-style, blue-collar, lower middle-class person.

By their paling faces, Georgie's two best friends in the world were starting to believe that Nat had known their best friend quite well.

"Um... tell her, tell her—" Georgie was behind Nat the whole way and kept throwing out tidbits she could use. "Liz is afraid that her threesome romp might show up on the Internet— the one with Ta—"

Nat coughed at threesome news before continuing, "She wouldn't dream of telling me anything personal about you. Georgie was very protective of her friends' privacy."

Not five minutes later, there was a collective sigh of relief from the ghosts when Nat entered the house and now stood in the middle of the foyer with Georgie's best friends.

"I know that pink was her favorite color." Nat touched her shirt, making Liz and Dahlia sniff in the sad memory. "She only told me about herself and what wonderful friends the three of you were."

Georgie passed through the exterior wall of the house into the foyer and her clothes changed. Gone was the cashmere sweater and light brown skirt, replaced by a floor-length black dress and some sort of pink coat, shawl thing that was feathery or furry, Nat couldn't tell which. What it really looked like was a swirl of cotton candy floating around her shoulders.

"Look at me!" Georgie squealed and she reached to her head, feeling her hair that was swept up and back in a fancy twist. "Just look at me. I'm beautiful."

Georgie looked as if she were on her way to a grand party, not on her way to being buried.

"They chose this dress for me. I *know* it. I just know it. Oh, thank you. Thank you, Dahlia, Liz." Georgie opened her arms to hug them but, of course, couldn't. They passed right through her.

"You picked the dress she's laid out in, didn't you?" Nat had to keep feeding them information to make it sound as if she and Georgie had been close. "You two are the only ones she'd trust. I can just imagine her in something dramatic, elegant. A long, black silk dress, maybe."

"How did you know?" Dahlia gasped.

"I really think that's the way she would have wanted it," Nat said decisively. "And she'd wear something fun. A shock of pink—a fur, a wrap, I don't know." She shrugged. "And then you'd make sure that her hair and makeup were done to perfection as if she were going out for a night on the town."

Liz and Dahlia teared up again. Nat had said what it took to convince them of her friendship with Georgie.

"You *have* to come with us," Liz announced, waving Skinner aside. Dahlia linked arms with Nat, creating a bond of acceptance. Offering friendship, however shallow.

"They've forgotten my purse." Georgie sounded panicked. "I can't be buried without a bag."

"And of course," Nat continued as if the idea had just come out of the blue to her. "You would have never forgotten the most important accessory. Georgie wouldn't have felt completely together without a purse."

"Her bag?" Dahlia mouthed. Her eyes grew wide with shock.

Liz turned to Dahlia who looked back horror-struck. "No, I didn't think— She wouldn't need—"

"I'm going straight up to her room right now." Dahlia dropped Nat's arm and ran toward the stairs.

Skinner unclipped and pulled aside the velvet cord, blocking the staircase, allowing Dahlia to pass.

"I want my gold-beaded Armani bag with the black tassel," Georgie called out to Dahlia as if she could hear her.

"How about the gold-beaded Armani bag?" Nat suggested, passing on the request.

Dahlia paused at the top landing and stared down at Nat. "The one with the tassel?"

Georgie nodded.

"That's the one," Nat confirmed, trying to sound as if being buried without one's favorite purse meant the end of the world.

"Perfect choice." Dahlia mimicked Georgie's nod and dashed out of sight.

"It's no wonder you and Georgie got along so well." Liz smiled, her face relaxed. "You have her taste."

"Not the same taste," Nat corrected. "Let's just say I get a clear message about what she would like."

"What am I going to do without these two?" Georgie sobbed, swiping at the tears rolling down her cheeks.

Nat felt bad for Georgie, it was the end of the world as she knew it. If she wanted her purse, Nat shouldn't be making jokes about it, even to herself.

Dahlia returned with the small gold-beaded purse and handed it to Liz who undid the clasp and looked inside. "This is where her Dynamic-Georgie perfume went. She'd been looking all over for it."

"So that's where it was." Georgie sounded relieved. "Who knew? After all this time?"

"That's been missing since before the Milan Spring show."

Dahlia replaced it in the purse. "I think we should leave it in there. She would want it with her."

What kind of perfume was Dynamic-Georgie? Nat had never heard of that brand before and she kept her mouth shut lest it give her away.

"It was the last personal perfume Daddy had made for me before he... he... died."

"Liz is so thoughtful," Georgie sniffed and looked like she was going to need a tissue.

Nat pulled her monogrammed "N" handkerchief from her purse and handed it to Liz. "Here. Put this in, too. From me."

"That's sweet, Natalie." Liz smiled.

Dahlia opened her tiger-print purse and pulled out a tube of lipstick. "Here—" she handed it to Liz "—It's Georgie's Pouty Lips in case she needs to reapply."

"My favorite custom lipstick."

"Good thinking," Nat whispered encouragingly, while mentally scratching her head, wondering what on earth Dahlia could be thinking about a deceased Georgie needing to reapply her lipstick.

———

DAHLIA HAD TAKEN care of Georgie's purse while Liz pulled Nat further into the house.

"I've never been here before," Nat explained, hesitant to move forward now that she'd made it past the butler. The service was in a large room, one nicely decorated. Presently, it held a podium and the flower-draped casket to the right and, lined up in front of it, rows and rows of mostly-occupied chairs.

"Why is my service in the front parlor?" Georgie did not sound pleased at all.

Nat spotted Mitch, who sat in the back of the room, waving them over.

"You can sit with us, we're in the front row," Liz told Nat. In the complete opposite direction from Mitch.

"You know," Nat said, uncertain of which way she should head. "I think I'll try and keep a low profile if that's all right with you. I feel sort of out of place. I don't know any of these people."

Liz had no objections. "Dahlia and I will meet up with you after the service, okay?" She gave Nat's hand one last squeeze before letting her go.

Nat headed to the left, followed by Georgie and Simon, who had just reappeared to join them as they moved toward Mitch.

"Oh, there's Anton Torvalli and Margie Lacegetter. Mr. Foxworthy is my father's old friend." Georgie pointed out as they passed a few people. "I can't quite see across the room. How many people are here?"

"It's a full house, Georgie," Simon told her. "I don't know who they are but they all look nice. Dark suits, professionally tailored, and expensive cuts. Very nice. The women are in tasteful, muted tones, nothing too flashy except for Tiger Lady over there." He pointed to Dahlia who stood at the front of the room.

"If we may now begin," a man in a somber suit, standing next to the casket intoned.

"What?" Georgie must have sensed the quieting of the crowd and glanced around. "What's going on now?"

"I think he's going to speak." Simon kept his attention riveted straight ahead.

"Who? Who is it?" Georgie persisted.

"Paul Russell," Nat said.

"I don't know who that is." Georgie didn't look very happy.

"He's the director of the Gates of Heaven Funeral Home." Nat read from the program.

"A funeral director? Yuck." Georgie wasn't pleased. "Why

can't one of my friends say something? How about my personal shopper or my scent designer?"

"We are here today to pay our last respects to Georgette Victoria Price," Russell began. "Georgette was young and beautiful and had a zest for living."

"Zest, huh?" Mitch shot a glance at Nat.

She didn't know what he was thinking but it couldn't have been anything good with that smirk on his face.

"Following the recent death of her father, George Victor Price, his daughter Georgette had been inspired to follow in his footsteps, designing her own line of cosmetics and fragrances and making Victor's of Paris the popular company it once was in the 1970s."

"What is he saying now?" Georgie nudged Simon.

"Her abrupt, early departure so soon after the untimely demise of her father...."

"Your father owned Victor's of Paris?" Simon gasped and couldn't hide that it impressed him.

"That's where he made his fortune—Ninja men's cologne," Russell continued. "'For the man who wants to conceal his intentions until he's ready to make his move.'"

"Who are you kidding?" Simon guffawed. "You could smell Ninja a mile away."

Georgie stared daggers at him. It seemed she hadn't appreciated his snide put-down.

"But then again," he amended with a polite cough and a forced smile. "It was popular at the time."

"And it made him rich," Georgie said as if that's all that really mattered.

"But his daughter Georgette was just as inventive in her own right."

"*Georgette*? Why does he keep calling you *Georgette*?" Mitch frowned.

"Because he doesn't know me."

"Even before her father's unfortunate passing, Georgette struggled to follow in her father's footsteps. She wanted to do it on her own terms and had her own ideas about bringing Victor's of Paris into the twenty-first century."

"Oh, come on. I'm bored." Georgie stood. "Let's go."

Go? You can't leave in the middle of your own funeral.

"Come on, Natalie," Georgie urged.

Nat couldn't leave as easily as they could . She moved to the doorway to the back of the room as inconspicuous as she could. Several guests glared at her inappropriate departure.

"I want to see my room." Georgie had lost all interest in her service and the phony praise this stranger was lavishing upon her. "Did they leave it exactly the way I left it?"

Nat had no idea and she wasn't keen to find out.

"No way to tell. We'll just have to see for ourselves." Simon escorted Georgie down the hall, Mitch followed and Nat brought up the rear.

"The butler's guarding the stairs." Simon stopped before Nat stepped out into the open.

"Don't worry, Skinner will let us through." Georgie smiled, giving an impatient sigh.

"He might have let you through, but he can't see you, and he's not going to let me walk down there by myself," Nat explained.

"That way." Georgie's smile was gone. She pointed straight down the hallway that disappeared into the darkness. "To Daddy's library. There's a secret staircase in there. You can sneak up that way. All you have to do is push one of the books to open the door."

"Which book?" Simon whispered back.

"Hmm... a big one," Georgie replied. "This is the library."

Nat placed her hand lightly upon the handle and turned. "Forget it, the door's locked."

"I remember the name of the book. It's *Seven*—something-something by T— E— La— or Le— or Lo— somebody."

"It's locked?" A smile tugged at the corner of Mitch's mouth. "I'll take care of it." He passed through the door to the other side. Nat felt her stomach leap into her throat. She'd never get used to seeing anyone pass through a wall.

Metallic clicks came from the lock assembly, someone... was unlocking the door. Mitch? Nat tried the handle again and the door opened. She glanced around before quickly slipping inside.

"How did you do that?" Simon remarked, obviously amazed.

"I thought you couldn't touch anything— real, solid." Nat couldn't believe it.

"I've learned to do a few tricks. I've been around for a while, remember?" Mitch gave a modest shrug. "Now where's this book?" He moved past the desk, toward the bookshelves on the walls that surrounded him.

"This is it," Georgie said, but her voice grew uncertain and hollow.

"I know, but which bookcase is it?" Mitch scanned the titles from left to right.

"This is the place. The spot where I... where I...." She stopped. And if a ghost could pale, then that's what she did. Georgie looked horrible—her coloring, her expression. Something beyond death passed over her.

"Take it easy, honey. What's happening?" Simon paused and watched Georgie very closely.

As if in some sort of trance, Georgie sat at the near end of a bolstered leather davenport. Simon held Georgie's hand and sat next to her, clearly concerned.

"It happened here. Right here." Georgie's eyes widened. It seemed she was having trouble breathing.

"Don't force yourself," Simon advised. "Just let it wash over you. It will. Take it easy." He turned to Nat and whispered, "The first time is always the worst."

"What's happening?" Nat whispered to Mitch. She could feel that something important, almost ritualistic, was happening before her. Something like an evolution process for the dearly departed.

Mitch stepped toward Nat and whispered, "She's reliving her death."

"I was sitting right here. It was after dinner. Late. I don't know why I'm here... in Daddy's library." She couldn't seem to puzzle anything out in her confusion. "Then I heard something. Did I? Or did I know that something or someone was here? Then something's around my neck." Georgie pulled her hand from Simon and clasped her neck. "I can't breathe. I can't... It's choking me." Her eyes fluttered shut and she went slack, falling back against the sofa.

"Tough break, kid." Mitch leaned against the desk. "It happens to the best of us."

"Just because we don't have physical bodies doesn't mean we can't feel it—the pain—in here." Simon pounded his chest with his fist for effect. "Reliving one's death is a harrowing experience."

Shouldn't be as bad as the real thing.

"You'll be okay, Georgie." Simon used soothing tones to bring her around.

Georgie pulled in a raspy breath.

"But does she know who did it?" Nat didn't want to sound insensitive to Georgie's reenacted death experience but if they could just find out that one little thing....

"Don't think so. Not yet." Mitch shrugged. "But she'll get more each time."

"More what? And what do you mean by each time?" It happened more than once? Nat hoped it wasn't over and over again, non-stop.

"You can't help but obsess about how you bite the big one." Mitch sounded like it was old news. "But you get over it soon enough."

"Excuse me." A man stepped into the room, interrupting. "What are you doing in here?" His voice wasn't immediately familiar but instant recognition hit when Nat saw him standing at the doorway.

"*Powell*... Natalie Powell?" he sounded as confused as she felt.

Daine Owens? Dressed in a dark suit, white shirt, and tie, it was the first time Nat had seen him without a chef's hat. What was he doing here?

"Oh, my God." Georgie sat bolt upright, looking like she'd seen a ghost. "It's my brother."

6

"BROTHER?" SIMON ECHOED then gawked at Georgie. "You have a brother?"

Mitch shot him a look that said, simply, *Duh*.

Simon, bursting with excitement, would have scribbled it down on a pad of paper just like one of those TV police detectives if he'd had a pad. "He's got to be one of the prime suspects."

Daine wasn't bald as Nat had thought when she first saw him. She wasn't sure which was more shocking, the family connection or that Daine had a dark, thick head of hair. It framed his eyes, bringing out their rich espresso-like color.

"He looks *delicious*." It seemed that Simon had forgotten about Georgie's pain and was nearly beside himself with delight, staring at Daine without shame, stating the obvious.

"He looks evil," Georgie said in a rush, gasping. "He has a goatee like a villain."

Nat could understand both statements. Daine's presence was completely unexpected and he looked so out of his element. To peg Nat's shock meter, he was Georgie's brother. Nat wondered about what the other little secrets he might be hiding.

"What are you doing in here?" Daine glanced around the room

as if he expected to see someone else. He must have thought that Nat was up to no good.

And she couldn't disagree. Nat had been an uninvited guest, wandering around a stranger's house. Yes, she had no business here on the Price property or in the library.

"Watch it, *doll*," Mitch warned, getting all protective. "I can see that he's a shifty character. You'd better keep your eyes on him."

"Don't let him know that you know who he is other than an ex-pain-in-the-ass boss. Don't tell him anything," Simon advised.

"Say that you were looking for the powder room." The words flew out of Georgie's mouth so fast Nat could tell it had surprised her.

"I was looking for the powder room," Nat repeated, much calmer than Georgie's delivery. "I must have gotten lost. It's a big house."

"I thought this room was locked." Daine's eyes narrowed. "We didn't want guests wandering around the house."

"Until I took care of it." With a raise of his eyebrows and knowing smile, Mitch blew on his fingertips and rubbed them against the lapel of his jacket.

"When I turned the handle, it was open." Which had been the truth.

"I'll see you to the *powder room* myself, then." He must have figured that Nat wasn't causing trouble and let it drop. The neutral line of his mouth was probably as close as he ever got to a smile.

Nat followed Daine out of the library and down the hall, passing two doors. "There you go." He pointed at the third door.

"Thanks," Nat said in the most gracious tone she could manage.

"Refreshments are being served out back." By a jerk of his head, he indicated the direction. "If you're okay finding that by yourself. Do you want me to wait? I can show you the way just in case you get lost again."

Nat opened the door and stepped inside, never taking her eyes off him. "No, that's all right. I'm sure I can find it just fine. Thanks, again." She smiled, closing the door and locking it. Safe at last.

The powder room consisted of a sofa, an overstuffed chair, and a small table on one side of a half-walled, professionally interior-decorated area. Nat peered through the archway to check out the other side. It hid the unsightly toilet and vanity. The whole space was bigger than her living room.

So this was how the other half lived?

Nat turned back toward the sofa in time to see Simon followed by Mitch and Georgie passed through the door she'd just closed.

"There's something fishy about him," Georgie started up. "I don't really remember him much, but I do know he's my brother, and I don't like him. I think he might be in marketing or something. Financial advisor? Stockbroker? I know... he's a salesman."

"He's a chef," Mitch told Georgie, setting the record straight.

"You can't let him know that you know anything more than you're supposed to know," Simon continued clearly all worked up. "If you start talking about things you ought not to know, some-one's going to start pointing a finger at you."

"All right, everyone, just keep your shirts on," Mitch, the voice of reason, said over them both.

"Excuse me," Nat waited for them to stop.

"Oh." Simon closed his mouth and glanced around, admiring the decor. "This is nice. Did you have this professionally done?"

"Yes, I did. I used Flora Goletta at Flora Designs. She did do a wonderful job in the front downstairs powder room, didn't she?" Georgie just had to distinguish the front downstairs powder room from the rear, main, east or west one, didn't she?

Nat got the point. She knew exactly what was meant. Georgie had money. She was rich.

"He's still out there, you know." Mitch, who remained cool, told Nat. "What are you going to do?"

"Who? Daine?" For a few seconds, Nat considered hiding here until the other guests had left but she was fairly sure she wouldn't get away with it.

"You have to get out there and mingle with the others," Georgie insisted.

Mingle. Talking to a bunch of strangers and occupying the same square mile with her most hated person on the planet? Nat couldn't imagine something she'd rather not do more.

"He's gone now, the coast is clear. We can move forward." Mitch reported, sounding like the military man he used to be.

Nat knew she had to do it. Had to—especially if she wanted to get rid of these guys. She opened the door, stepped out, down the hall, through the front parlor, toward the back of the house. This didn't look much like a back yard, more like a miniature Versailles garden.

A smooth, natural stone patio extended from the house. Off on either side of the house, extending from the patios were manicured gardens. Straight back sat a freeform pool with a two-story waterfall and the pool house, although they'd probably call it a cabaña.

At the moment there were dozens of tables dotting the patio. There was nothing sad or dreary about the way they'd been decorated. Crisp, white tablecloths with a three-foot high flower arrangement sat in the center of each table set with apricot and pastel yellow plates. Gleaming sterling silver cutlery adorned the tops alongside elaborately folded napkins. Nat might have mistaken this get-together for a birthday party or an equally festive occasion.

"There they are!" Georgie stood on tiptoe and waved. "Lizzy! Dahlia!"

As if they'd responded to Georgie's hail, the two young ladies waved, not to Georgie but to Nat to join them. Nat made her way across the patio to a rather choice location, she thought, by the koi pond where a soft, cool breeze passed.

"You weren't talking to who I thought you were talking to, were you?" Dahlia had the most unpleasant expression. She hadn't any idea that Nat had been speaking with ghostly Georgie, had she?

"Who would that be?" Nat wondered who could be so hated in their eyes.

"Daine Owens," was spoken through two sets of absolutely straight and unnaturally white teeth.

Nat didn't have to guess, Daine had been the only *person* she'd spoken to besides Skinner since she'd crashed the memorial service.

"I'd swear he must have had something to do with it," Dahlia muttered in a low, hate-filled tone. "Georgie's... death."

"See, I told you." Simon elbowed Mitch. The trio had pulled up seats over the koi pond, hovering a few feet over the surface.

Mitch stood. "I'm going to go scout around." He bent to whisper in Nat's ear. "Let me know if anything worthwhile happens, will ya?"

Nat managed to meet his gaze for an instant to let him know she understood.

"You don't know that, Dahlia." Liz made a surreptitious glance in Owens' direction.

Nat was no fan of his. Yeah, he was a terror in the kitchen, but she really had a hard time believing he could have killed anyone... outside a kitchen, that is.

"You can never tell what someone is capable of, especially when there's a lot of money at stake." Dahlia sounded certain she knew who'd done Georgie in.

"They got close to nothing when their father died," Liz told Nat ever-so-casually. "Who knows, maybe they're in on it together."

"*They*?" Nat stopped, glancing between the two and settled her attention on Liz.

"The brothers. Could have been either of them, maybe both of them." Liz picked up her champagne glass and took a sip.

"I have *two* brothers?" Georgie blinked, amazed to hear the details of her life. "I can't remember."

"Each got a measly fifty thousand or so," Liz continued. "Just enough so they couldn't make an issue over Georgie's inheritance. But Georgie didn't think it was fair. She thought they deserved more."

Dahlia glanced at Liz, her eyes welling up. "Georgie was so amazing."

Georgie sniffed, holding back her own tears.

"That's why she had them over for dinner that night. She was going to give them the good news." Dahlia set her glass on the table and picked up her tiger-print purse. "I bet that even a third of an empire isn't good enough for one of them."

"I was so kind, so thoughtful, so generous." Georgie sobbed and popped open her purse to delve inside.

"One of them must have come back. After dinner, after the staff retired."

"But how?" Nat imagined as close friends to Georgie, almost family, they knew more details than the general public. Since they were Georgie's best friends, maybe they knew more than the police.

"They broke a window, forcing their way into the house, and then they stabbed her." Dahlia voiced in dramatic tones.

"They tried to make it look like a break-in. Like some criminal did it," Liz added.

"That way the two brothers could split it all in half." Dahlia seemed to have it all worked out.

Except— *Stabbed her?* That wasn't how Georgie had died.

"That's terrible." Georgie wailed, not realizing the major flaw of Dahlia's story—the wrong cause of death. From her sequined purse, Georgie pulled out a handkerchief to wipe her tears.

Nat's breath caught when she saw the monogrammed 'N' of her own handkerchief in Georgie's hand. The fact was, someone had killed Georgie and if Dahlia was right, Daine and his brother both had a very good motive to want their sister dead.

"I SEE YOU'VE found your way to the party." Daine Owens stood next to Nat before she could say *al dente*.

What had she done to deserve his attention?

"Yeah, I was sitting with Liz and Dahlia, over there." Nat motioned toward the pond while trying to sound pleasant like she was having a good time.

"Oh, those two." By his tone, Nat figured he didn't think much of them. "They're on permanent jet lag. Talk about ditzy."

Nat glanced around, making sure Georgie wasn't nearby. She wouldn't let him get away with talking about her 'two best friends in the whole wide world' like that.

"I just met them today." Nat finally spotted Georgie sitting with Liz and Dahlia. "They're her friends— they *were* her friends."

"Sour grapes," Simon interjected, appearing in a chair close by. "Probably struck out with both of them, I'd say. They wouldn't even give him the time of day."

Nat didn't even flinch when he materialized out of nowhere. She kept her focus on the man before her.

"Yeah, *Georgie*." He didn't sound as if he wanted to talk about her. "How did you know her?"

"You've already had this pop quiz once," Simon warned. "Don't blow it now."

"Stick to your story, *doll*." Mitch appeared in a chair opposite Simon. The two of them looked like they had ringside seats to the awkward tableau. "You don't want to be caught lying."

"She was looking for a new personal chef," Nat answered without hesitation.

"You mean she was going to get rid of Alberto?" Daine sounded hurt. "He's been here forever... well, he's outlasted all of my father's marriages."

"Your father?" This was the first mention of his family ties to Georgie.

"Georgette was my half-sister, you know." The use of her full name and the tone he used told Nat that they weren't close.

"Now we're getting somewhere." Simon rubbed his hands together. "Come on, get him to tell you some of the dirty family secrets."

"Daine," a woman's voice separated them, ending their momentary closeness. "Is this a new girl you're with?"

"She's not bad looking for an older broad." Mitch couldn't quite keep the leer out of his voice.

"Mom," Daine took a half step away from Nat, making room for an attractive older blonde-haired woman. "This is Natalie Powell."

"Nat, this is Marian Price."

"Ooooh, the ex-wife." Simon gloated. "She's bound to have some scintillating secrets to add."

"Nice to meet you, Mrs. Price." Nat found it easier to be civil to her, a perfect stranger, than to Daine, a detested co-worker.

"Please, call me Marian." Marian seemed very polite, likable. How did she ever end up with an overbearing jerk like Daine for a son? And why, by the way, was his last name Owens when it should have been Price? That's what Nat wanted to know. "And it's very nice to meet you."

Marian turned to Daine. "Why don't you bring her to dinner tomorrow night so I can get to know her better?" She had sort of a hungry look in her eye as if she'd found the perfect woman for her son.

Nat found Marian's attention disturbing. She didn't like the future-girlfriend vibe she was getting.

Daine hemmed and hawed, looking as awkward as he sounded. "I'm sure she's working," he said to his mother then turned to Nat. "Are you?"

"No, I'm not." Why couldn't Nat just lie about that? Did she say that just to be contrary?

"Easy fact to check," Mitch chimed in. "Good thing you told the truth."

"I'm certain your brother and Alice would love to meet her." Marian sounded very pleased and was doing her best to encourage both of them to comply.

"Natalie?" Daine said with a shrug. She could hardly blame him either, he was trapped in the matchmaking-scheme as well, whether he liked it or not.

"This is it." Mitch pointed out if anyone had missed this gaping hole of an opportunity. "Here's your *in* if you want to find out more."

"You've got to go, Natalie." Simon perched on the edge of his chair. "You've just got to."

It felt as if a minute or ten of silence had passed before she answered.

Under normal conditions, she'd never, ever plan to spend time with him voluntarily, but this time... this time she had to admit that Simon was right. This was her chance, maybe the only one.

"Thank you, Marian," Nat said then turned to her one-time, dreaded co-worker. "Daine, I'd love to."

WORK THAT NIGHT was heaven. For an evening Nat could forget about Daine, forget about the ghosts, and concentrate on something she loved—cooking. When she got home she fell into bed and into a deep sleep.

"Come on," Simon's voice prodded. "Rise and shine, sleepyhead!"

"Huh?" Nat grunted and with an enormous effort managed to raise her head off her pillow. "What time is it?"

"Ten, I think." Simon didn't sound as cheery breaking that news to her.

"Ten in the morning?" Nat said in disbelief.

"You should have let her sleep until at least noon." Georgie's voice of experience with a hint of I-told-you-so scolded him.

"I'd kill you if you weren't already dead." Nat rubbed her eyes, trying to wake. She heard Simon's audible gasp at her threat.

"I tried to tell you this was too early." Thankfully, Mitch's voice sounded as if it were coming from across the room and not next to her.

"Get out, all of you!" Nat, feeling tired and grumpy, sat up and waved them away. "Get out!"

Almost a half hour later she emerged from her room dressed but still feeling grouchy.

"I would have made a pot of coffee but—" Mitch's hand passed right through the handle of the coffee pot.

Sure—locks he could open but he was useless when it came to making coffee.

"I would have, too, but I don't know how." Georgie might have wanted to sound helpful but she came across as being pathetic.

Nat turned to Simon who sat in the overstuffed chair. "And don't you have something to say?"

"I think you should get right to what you'll be wearing tonight." Simon must have known what he was good at and decided to stick to that.

"It's not even eleven." Nat couldn't believe what she was hearing.

"Simon's right, you have to pick out your outfit." Georgie had made a quick switch from coffee to clothing. "Daine's going to be here at four."

"I think I can manage to throw something together in five hours," Nat said, it came out sounding angry.

Another gasp from Simon. "That's exactly what we don't want —something *thrown* together." He pushed out of the chair. "You need to think about what you want to achieve. Your purpose." He gestured with his hands, his arms, trying to create a bigger, higher meaning.

"I don't want to spend any time with him. I want to get home as quick as I can," Nat said truthfully.

"You're not going for yourself, you're going for *Georgie*. Or have you forgotten?" Simon got serious. "You need to find out more about the brothers. What are they like? Are they capable of murder?"

That woke Nat up. He was right. Her "date" with Daine wasn't supposed to be torture. It was a job, a mission, something to be tolerated. Nat, with the help of her cohorts, would find out if either or both of Georgie's brothers were greedy enough to commit murder.

"*Dress for success* are not just words, they're a direction, guidance." Simon enlightened Nat. "You want to be received into their home and fit in. You want them to feel comfortable with you. Comfortable enough to open up and talk to you like they've known you forever. Tell you things they would never tell a stranger."

"Is that possible?" Before now Nat thought that Simon was off his rocker but now he was starting to make some sense. Maybe Nat was really beginning to lose her sanity.

"You have no idea." Georgie smiled, taking a place next to Simon, in more ways than just physically. "Its presentation like a delicious serving of food, making it look just right enhances the dining experience."

Georgie was right.

"I think with the two of us helping, we can do just that." Simon couldn't have sounded more enthusiastic.

"Oh, lucky you," Mitch said under his breath for only Nat to hear. She glanced at him and caught his smirk.

"Okay." Nat agreed. She could tell that they knew what they were talking about. "But can this wait until I've had some coffee and a piece of toast?"

Georgie and Simon acted as if they'd made another convert to their side and did a little celebration dance. "Sure, sure," they chorused.

Mitch looked thoroughly disgusted and shook his head. "While the three of you girls are playing dress up, I'll just take a hike." With that said, he winked and faded into nothingness.

"NEXT." SIMON MOTIONED with a wave of his hand to Nat to hurry.

She slid the garment on the hanger from the right to the left in her tiny closet.

"Next." He motioned again, and again Nat slid the hanger to the left. "Next."

"Don't you have anything but cotton tees and little summer shifts?" Georgie commented while seated on Nat's bed. "Don't you have anything suitable?"

"They're clothes. The restaurant provides working clothes. I don't need much more than that."

Simon froze and stared at Nat. "Is that what you really think? You need more help than I thought."

"I'm sorry if I don't have anything in my closet that might be—"

"Nat?" Becca's uncertain voice came through Nat's bedroom door followed by her reluctant appearance. "Are you okay?" She hovered at the doorway and glanced at Nat then around the room. "Who are you talking to?"

Gulp. "No one. Just taking a self-wardrobe evaluation poll out loud." Nat straightened in her awkwardness. "That's all. You know, getting a second and third opinion from *Me*, who thinks I could use something dressier, and *Myself*, who thinks I need a complete wardrobe overhaul." She nodded and motioned to her closet. "*I* seem to think I'm stuck with what's here and there isn't any time to do anything about it."

"What are you looking for?"

"Something for a dinner date."

"You have a date?" Becca sounded beyond shocked. "With a man? When did this happen? Who is he? When did you meet him? *How* did this happen?" She came into the room, eager for details and eased onto the bed. To prevent from being sat on, Georgie blinked out of sight.

"At the funeral." Nat got the impression Becca wasn't going to leave until she got answers so she'd better start talking. And her sister didn't have to sound so surprised. Nat met men. Sometimes. And she went on dates. Sometimes.

"You met a guy at a funeral? Eww." Becca screwed up her face. If Nat had taken a moment to listen to herself, she'd have realized that meeting someone at a funeral didn't sound too good. A little on the gross side.

"I didn't meet him there. I already knew him. Daine Owens." Saying his name out loud cemented the reality of it.

A date with Daine. Ugh.

"Not *that* guy." Becca sounded puzzled. Her smile dropped when she met Nat's gaze. "Didn't you just interview for a job with him?"

"That's right."

"I thought you didn't like him. And you have a date with him?"

"It's just dinner."

"Okay. I think it's weird." Becca shook her head. "If you're willing to 'go out to dinner with him' just for a...so you can..."

"No, it isn't like that." There was nothing she could say to make this sound better. "This has nothing to do with the job."

"You know, it's none of my business." Becca stood. "I just stopped by to pick up my coat."

"What are you doing here, then?" Nat wanted her sister to leave and stop thinking that she was nuts. "Is he waiting for you? Theo?"

"Oh, yeah." Becca raced out of the room and thumped around in the hall closet. Her footsteps grew louder and she reappeared at Nat's bedroom door. "Go ahead and look through my clothes, you'll find something. Wait a minute—I just bought a skirt and a top you can borrow. They still have the tags on them. I'm sure they'll be perfect."

"I'll be the judge of that." Simon snipped at Becca, even though she couldn't hear him.

"You can tell me about your date later. I gotta go." Becca dashed off and Nat heard the front door close with a resounding bang.

"Thanks." Nat waved after her sister had left.

Simon clapped his hands together. "Quick we haven't a moment to lose—to Becca's closet!"

7

"*VA-VA-VA VOOM!*" SIMON'S eyes went wide when he saw Nat step out of her bedroom.

"I got two words for you," Simon said with his index and middle fingers raised, and he shook his head in a slow and deliberate manner. "*Lamb. Chops.* I don't want to say 'I told you so' but *I told you so.*"

"Fits a bit snugly but overall it works," Georgie gave Natalie the once over for the thousandth time but she seemed pleased with the overall effect. "Remember, you never get a second chance to make a first impression. You want to get this right."

Nat could hardly believe the reflection that stared back at her was her own. Becca's new outfit was cute, nudged toward the sexy side by the way it hugged her body.

Her once straight, shoulder-length hair now framed her flawless, glowing face with soft large, loose curls. Georgie knew exactly what she was doing. She'd given Nat detailed instructions on how to wield the curling wand and apply a little make-up, also borrowed from Becca, to perfection.

"How's that for warm and friendly, Mitch?" Simon turned to Mitch for a man's unbiased opinion. "Mitch?"

There was silence for a long time.

Then Mitch answered, "It's all right." But that's not what his body language said.

Nat swung her gaze from the mirror to Mitch. Was he blind? Even she could see the difference. A big difference. Maybe he didn't like what he saw. Sophisticated wasn't to his liking. Maybe he liked his woman more scantily clad and on the sleazy side.

Who cared what he liked anyway?

"You can't forget your bag, that'll finish the whole look." Georgie peered into the closet.

"How about this?" Nat snagged a coordinating purse she thought might do the trick.

"No." Georgie refused. "You're not going to a job interview."

Nat made a second choice; a small, glittering-with-something clutch and held it over her head for Georgie to see. "How about this one?"

"That bag does not fit the occasion."

Hand it to the Pocketbook Princess to give Nat a hard time about the perfect purse.

"All you need is something small, just large enough for your plastic, cell, and lipstick." Georgie ticked each off on her fingers.

Nat hadn't the heart to break it to Georgie that out of the three items she listed, all she had was the cell. The only plastic worth bringing was her driver's license, and she was pretty sure that wasn't what Georgie was talking about.

There was a knock at the front door. Nat glanced at the clock. Daine was early.

"I don't think I'm ready yet," she whispered, sounding panicked.

"You're fine, and you look fabulous." Simon assured her. "Go ahead and answer the door. We're all ready."

AS ALWAYS, THE trio did not travel by car. Nat was alone with Daine for the trip to his mother's. They drove out of San Bruno, past San Mateo and kept going south.

This whole thing was weird. Her and him. Together.

Daine?

In a car, together. Going to dinner.

It wasn't a date. It was more of a spy mission.

But dressed in a white crew shirt and dark blue jacket, he hardly resembled his old self. He actually looked handsome.

The words *handsome* and *Daine* should not have occupied the same thought.

The shock of seeing him without his chef's hat and the bigger shock of seeing him with all that dark hair, almost made her forget he was the same man she'd so detested if it weren't for his familiar close-cropped goatee.

They'd just passed through Redwood City and within moments rolled into Menlo Park. Nat glanced out the window at the small cream-colored bungalow with light brown trim.

"This is it." He put the car in park and set the parking brake.

"Is this the house you grew up in?"

"Since I was three." He turned off the engine and opened the driver's side door.

What he probably meant was since his parent's divorce.

Nat decided that maybe she'd better watch it. If she asked too many personal questions he might clam up which would make this outing worthless.

Daine opened her door. Once she stepped outside the car she realized they probably would no longer be alone. *They* would return. Nat took a steadying breath and braced herself. Tonight was not going to be easy.

"You look nice," he said.

"You've already said that." If Nat had been counting it might have been the eighth or ninth time he'd said it. Okay, she liked to hear it and she knew it was the ninth, but she didn't want to obsess over it.

"Well, I mean it. You look really nice." He smiled at her.

"Thanks." Nat smiled at Daine while he held the door open, surprising herself how easy it was to be nice to him. She squinted at his brand-spanking-new, Key lime green, retro-styled Ford Mustang. "Is this the car you won on the American Chef Challenge?"

"Did you see the show?" He sounded almost embarrassed.

"I try and catch it if I'm home," Nat said casually. In reality, she was glued to the set every week and never missed a single originally aired episode. "If I remember, you had the sockeye salmon theme."

"I thought Bobby Flay was going to skin and filet me. I don't know how I did it but somehow I managed to out grill the grill master." Daine knocked on the front door before letting himself in.

During the show, he had created five dishes. Puff pastry-wrapped salmon and watercress mousse with champagne-chive butter Sauce for an appetizer and a smoky salmon chowder. For his main entrée, he'd kabobbed various vegetables with chunks of salmon and served them *à la Daine*.

He'd scored mega points with a sauce he'd whipped up and drizzled over the fish. Then he'd prepared pan-seared salmon with peanuts over crispy noodles and Asian greens as a side dish.

For dessert, there was lemon sorbet with crispy salmon flakes sprinkled on top. Each dish was as wonderful to look at as it was to taste, and if the viewers were to believe the celebrity judges, each dish was a unique, flavor-filled experience.

Nat followed Daine through the front door

"Hello, there." A nice looking man approached. And unknown to him, just inside the house appeared three additional, uninvited guests.

Nat only saw the back of Simon and Georgie's heads while Mitch smiled and waved at her, pulling his hat off his head.

"Nat, this is my brother Greg." The sound of Daine's voice next to her nearly made Nat jump.

"Greg. I remember Greg," Georgie said fondly from behind him. Her eyes crinkled when she smiled.

"Hi, Greg." Nat had to force herself to pay attention to Greg and not look past him.

"Nat—Natalie, right?" He held out his hand for her to shake. "Nice to meet you. Please, come in."

"What's with the friendly nice-to-see-you bit? He could be the murderer, you know." Simon gawked at Greg while standing next to him then rolled his eyes. "Sheesh, you think his brother" — meaning Daine— "never brought a girl home before."

Nat walked past Greg into the house. Daine closed the front door behind them and she heard the brother whisper, "Finally," in a telling, approving wink-wink tone.

"Oh, my word! He *has* never brought a girl home before." Simon announced in pure astonishment after studying Greg's expression. "I bet he's a virgin, too."

Simon moved his penetrating stare from Greg to Daine, maybe waiting to see if the letters: V-I-R-G-I-N would appear on his forehead.

"Is there a place I can hang my jacket?" Nat asked a bit too forcefully. She wanted to move away from Simon's dismal topic and reintegrate herself with the world of the living. Nat really had to do her best to ignore him, all of them, and pay attention to the people around her.

Daine led Nat to the hall closet and made some comment. She supposed he was trying to be funny, about her getting lost while looking for the powder room in the Price mansion. Nat had her attention focused on Mitch who dropped his hat on the coffee table.

"We'll leave Natalie to talk to the suspects while we have a look around. Remember, we only have one shot at this so everyone" — he glanced from Georgie to Simon and leaned forward for a private word— "Pay attention. Keep your eyes and ears open. On the plus side, we can go anywhere and take our time checking things out. On the con side, we can only skim the surface. We can't delve into drawers or search through any personal items. Do your best. Now spread out."

"Did you want a tour of the house, Nat?" Daine's voice was on the loud side.

"Yes, you do," Mitch instructed her. "If you're not there, we can't go there, either."

"What?" Nat should have been paying more attention to her area—the suspects—as Mitch had put it. She was having a hard time listening to two conversations at once.

"A house tour?" Daine repeated. "Did you want one? Outside you seemed interested in having a look at—"

"Yes," she said, taking Mitch's lead. "That would be great."

"Daine!" a woman's voice called from another room. "Mom wants you to start the gravy."

Daine glanced from Nat to the back of the house. He clearly looked torn, almost as if he didn't want to leave her. "That's weird because the women usually don't allow me in the kitchen."

"But they *always* ask him to make a sauce or gravy if they need it." A side of Greg's mouth hitched up into a smile. "He won't give them the secret."

"Go make the gravy. Greg can walk me through if that's all right." Nat suggested, glancing at him.

"No problem. It'll be a short tour, it's a small house." Greg sounded almost bitter. But why should he? This is where he grew up, too.

"I'll just be in the kitchen if you need me," Daine said, sounding a little left out.

"You might not see us, but we'll be around." Mitch shimmered from sight.

Greg motioned to the living room. "The house is old, built in the fifties."

This house was, Nat thought, usually tidy, maybe because Marian Price knew she was having company. Every flat surface held picture frames.

All the pictures, with the exception of wedding photos on the table at the front of the house, were of the brothers. The brothers as young men at home for the holidays and sightseeing while on vacation. Those on the wall looked like pictures from high school.

Built-in bookcases flanked the small brick fireplace. On the right side of the mantle were photos of Greg in several incarnations of cap and gown and on the left were Daine in different chef's uniforms adorned with various medals and holding trophies. Most notably the distinctive wide red ribbon with a bronze medallion hanging around his neck with the caption: *James Beard Foundation, Rising Star Chef of the Year.*

Nat couldn't help but be impressed.

"This way to the rest of the house." Greg motioned toward the hall.

The hallway wall was lined with grade school pictures. Nat felt this was a close family and Marian must have certainly loved her boys. However, she also noticed that not one picture of their father was anywhere to be seen.

At the end of the hall were two bedroom doors and a bathroom on the left.

"That was our room." Greg motioned .

Nat entered and took in an eyeful. Twin beds, a dresser, and several sports pennants and school certificates hung on the wall.

"I was the family jock. Basketball, baseball, soccer, you name it, I played it," Greg said with a definite I'm-better-than-my-brother air. "Daine never cared for sports, but you could always count on him to have dinner ready at home after practice." With a jerk of his head, Greg moved the tour on. "My mom's bedroom."

So Greg was the physical one and, even back then, Daine swung the spoon. Nat followed him into the next room. It was about the same size as the first room with a window on the right instead of the left and decorated more feminine.

A soft yellow covered the walls and a floral bedspread with pastel pillows accented the bed. Recent pictures of Daine and Greg, with his wife, sat on the nightstand along with Mitch Albom's book, *For One More Day.*

"We had a master bath and walk-in closet added some five years back."

Nat peeked through the bathroom door at the spacious master bath. Clearly a new addition, it was nearly as large as the bedroom.

"This way. I'll take you to what you no doubt think is the most important room in the house—the kitchen." Greg led the way, back the way they'd come and gestured with his arm. "This is supposed to be the dining room but it's the only place big enough for mom's piano."

A baby grand sat in the center of a room with a small bay window. Photos of the boys during the pre-school years sat on the closed lid of the piano.

Greg slid onto the piano bench and began to play some famous classical piece Nat had heard before. Beethoven? Mozart? He sounded amazingly good.

"What do you do for a living?" Thoughts of him playing at a piano bar crossed Nat's mind. Maybe he was moonlighting. Was Greg capable of murder?

"I'm a dermatologist."

A doctor. Nat figured he probably wasn't moonlighting, then.

"Daine doesn't play half as well as I do," Greg bragged without missing a note.

And he wasn't modest about it.

"Ten years of lessons, you'd think he could play Heart and Soul or at least pick out Chopsticks."

"I heard that!" Daine roared from the kitchen. "Stop showing off."

The music stopped and Greg laughed. "His talent isn't music, it's cooking. Me? I can't even boil water." He moved from the piano across the hall to the door and waved Nat to follow.

"*Voilà*. Behold the kitchen." Greg stepped aside. To Nat's surprise, a state-of-the-art kitchen stood in this 1950s house. A modern day cooktop, oven, refrigerator, and dishwasher were all integrated into a renovated period kitchen.

"There has to be a decent place to cook," Daine said, never taking his eyes off his saucepan while he stirred.

"You're not even supposed to be cooking, Mr. Big-Shot Chef," a woman scolded him.

"Nat, my wife, the lovely Alice."

"Nice to meet you, Nat." Alice looked over her shoulder and made a move as if she wanted to shake hands but they were filled with wet salad greens, she shrugged and smiled.

"And you, Alice. Thanks for inviting me, Mrs. Price." Nat said to the mother, whom she'd already met. She wondered if she should pitch in and help out with dinner.

"Please, call me Marian."

"Why isn't Daine allowed in the kitchen?" Was there a no-Daine rule or a general no-men rule?

"I don't expect Daine to come to dinner and have to cook for me," Marian explained. "He cooks for a living but not in my house except when it comes to a little gravy now and then. He has the most delicious sauces."

"Delicious isn't the right word for his creative kitchen concoctions." Alice was breathless just talking about it. She might have gotten a little glossed-eyed, too.

Curiosity got the best of her. Nat leaned toward Daine and peered into his saucepan.

"What do you have in there?"

"Liquid magic." He glanced at her and flashed a modest smile.

"What goes into it?" She whispered with interest, inspecting the color and thickness of the contents.

"It's *secret...*" —Daine's eyebrows rose and his voice grew cautious— "...liquid magic."

"You need to write a book, that's what you should do," Alice advised. "Everyone would buy it. You could make a fortune."

"But then it wouldn't be a secret anymore." He placed a very small bit of gravy onto Nat's palm.

Nat inhaled the complex aroma before tasting. It was heavenly. Rich and delicious. Alice was right, words alone did not do Daine's gravy justice. Nat's eyelids slid shut as she delighted in its perfection.

The last thing Nat remembered was sitting at the dinner table with the rest of the family and taking a bite of gravy-coated meat-loaf before blacking out from the taste of Daine's sauce's savory splendor.

MITCH LEANED AGAINST the wall behind Natalie with his arms crossed and watched the occupants of the dinner table. What made these people tick? Were any of them capable of murder? Hell, he figured anyone was capable, given the right motivation.

Simon appeared next to him. "What's going on? What did I miss?"

"Nothing much," Mitch grunted. "Just your regular Norman Rockwell family Sunday dinner."

"Norman Rockwell my ass, not unless Charles Manson is a

relative. One of those people is a cold-blooded killer." Simon eyed each person around the table carefully before going on to the next.

Mitch threw a skeptical glance at Simon. "I'm not going to even pretend to understand what that means."

"Just think of a crazed Al Capone." Simon did his best to put it into a time frame Mitch would understand.

Al Capone was a before Mitch's time but he got the message. "Where's Georgie?"

"She's in the back checking on something." Simon exhaled impatiently then flung out his hand, indicating Natalie. "Now, why isn't she asking those hard to answer questions?"

Natalie didn't react to Simon's outburst.

"That's because she's too busy feeding her face." Mitch cranked his volume up a couple of notches, making sure she would hear him. She should have.

Still no reaction.

"Well, why the heck did we bother coming here?" Simon huffed. "Was it to find out who killed Georgie or play house with the Prices?"

"I think she got sidetracked." It was pretty pathetic sounding but it was the truth. Natalie wasn't showing the slightest bit of interest in them.

"What could possibly taste so good that—" Simon stopped then continued wide-eyed. "Hey, maybe the food is drugged. Do you think?"

"Nah. They'd all be glassy-eyed or something." Mitch checked the expressions of the people around the table again. "Besides, what's the point?"

The diners ooh-ed and ahh-ed over their meatloaf like it was some special eats. Chow was never that good or maybe it'd had been too long since Mitch'd had a decent meal. Greg and his wife Alice praised the Great Daine, Master of the Sauce, with nearly every mouthful.

Humph, *The Great Daine*—that was a joke. What kind of a name was that? In Mitch's day, a Great Dane was a dog. Mitch didn't like the look of this guy. And he didn't like the way he looked at Natalie.

The meatloaf gravy didn't have the paralyzing effect on Daine that it had on the others. Mitch noticed how Daine paid careful attention to Natalie. There was the slightest softening in his eyes when he thought no one was watching.

He was wrong there, Buddy. Mitch was watching. Very closely.

"That was delicious, people. Thank you so much." Greg dabbed at the sides of his mouth with his napkin. "What's for dessert?"

"Dessert?" Alice slapped his arm. "How could you possibly eat anything else?"

"What a glutton!" Simon crowed.

"What you really mean is there's no dessert." Greg sounded almost angry. Was he the type of man to lose his cool because there wasn't any chocolate cake? Mitch wondered.

"Why must there be dessert?" Alice sounded a bit frustrated.

"The man ate enough to fill all four cow's stomachs." Simon gestured at Daine. "And that man's a complete pig."

Greg glanced toward Natalie and Daine, made an unpleasant face and said, "Store-bought cookies?"

"The boys usually like a nice home-baked pie or cake after dinner," Marian stated calmly, setting her knife and fork on her dinner plate.

"The *whole* pie or cake," Alice added. "Each. You have to make three if anyone else is having a piece."

"I don't have to listen to this abuse," Daine said in mock anger. He stood and began to collect the dinner dishes. He may have complained but he also must have known the faster the dishes were cleared the quicker dessert would be on the table.

"Greg?" Alice prompted. "Aren't you going to help?" But her husband sat there like a disgruntled lump.

"Why isn't Natalie doing something?" Simon fumed.

"About dessert or about them?" Mitch indicated the sweet-starved brothers.

"I can't get motivated, knowing there's only a bag of Keebler's in my future." Greg slouched, looking completely disappointed.

Alice rolled her eyes.

"Please," Natalie stood and held out her hand to stay Greg. "Let me help."

"It's about time." Simon huffed and finally calmed down. "Been sittin' there lettin' them wait on you hand and foot. What kind of guest are you?"

Mitch would have thought she'd have something to say about that, but she didn't.

"Sit down, Daine." Alice pulled the plates out of his hands. "Nat and I will take care of the dishes. We can't have you-boys too close to the lemon chiffon pie."

"Pie!" Greg straightened, wide-eyed, ready to launch out of his chair.

"Don't get too excited, there's only one for the five of us. So you'll have to limit yourselves."

"Come on, boys," their mother said. "Let's go into the living room and wait for dessert."

"You tell them, Mom. Get those good-for-nothings out of the way." Simon cheered Marian on.

"But we want to help clear the dinner dishes." Greg was on his feet, high-tailing it around the table, trying to collect plates, making a poor attempt at wrestling one out of Natalie's hands.

"That's it, fight him for it." Simon urged Natalie. "What is wrong with her?" He pointed at her with a puzzled expression. "I don't think she hears us anymore."

"There is no way you're getting near the kitchen." Alice

blocked Greg's way. "You'll have to wait until it's cut and on the table."

"Gregory—in the living room, now," Marian ordered. The men headed out, and Mitch followed. He wasn't about to let Daine out of his sight. Not for a second.

NAT HAD HEARD them, all right. But she was doing her best to keep focused on the family, the whole Price family. Who went where, what they did, and how they did it at home, at work or at play, all of it was discussed over the evening meal.

Listening to the weekly rundown of the family's comings and goings, Nat would never have guessed that these people, two of them specifically, might have been killers. They seemed so normal.

"Did you see those two men move? They've been trained right." Alice followed Nat to the kitchen sink. "Mom's done a wonderful job raising them. Especially considering she didn't have much help from their father."

"I know their parents were divorced but their father wasn't there for his boys at all?" Nat jumped at the chance to talk about George Price.

"All he gave then was minimal child support." Alice pulled out containers for the leftovers. "Mom had to work."

"But he had money, didn't he?" Nat scraped the leftover pieces off each plate and into the garbage can.

"George Victor Price did not share much. He was too busy with himself. His company, his wives, and his little girl. That's all he cared about."

"Wives? How many times was he married?"

"Three? Four? I'm not sure. Lots. He stopped after he had a girl with the last one." Alice opened the dishwasher and started to load the dishes. "He spent all his time doting on her. You'll notice that neither Greg nor Daine are named after him. He saved it for his daughter: Georgette Victoria Price. Will you get the plates for the pie?"

Nat pulled five dessert plates from the cabinet and five forks from the drawer.

"Daine's so bitter about it that he won't even use the Price last name. He goes by his mother's maiden name *Owens*."

"Does Greg hold the same grudge?"

"He seems to deal with it but he's always been tougher than his little brother."

"How long have you two been married?"

"Almost five years now." Alice closed the dishwasher and brought the pie from the refrigerator. "We met in medical school years before and went our separate ways after we graduated. It was such a shock when we ended up interning at the same place." Alice pulled the pie server out of a drawer. "I was surprised to hear that Daine was bringing someone tonight. He's dated a couple of girls but that never worked out. His career has always come first, but I guess you know all about that."

"We worked together a couple of years ago. I bumped into him at Georgie's service yesterday."

Alice froze in mid-slice at the mention of the half-sister's name.

"I take it neither of them was close to their sister." Nat kept a close watch on Alice's body language.

"They never met her until their father died six months ago." Alice sliced the first piece and placed it on a plate. "Greg told me she wanted to talk about their father's estate and his will. She didn't think the will was fair, wanted to give the brothers more money."

"She did?" That surprised Nat. She had the idea that Georgie was more self-centered than that. "That seems pretty nice."

"*Nice* must run in the family, then." Alice dished out the fifth piece and placed it on the plate. "Daine has a *nice* streak a mile wide. Greg has one, too. His is a little harder to see but it's there."

"Then maybe next time" —if there ever were a next time— "they'll let me help in the kitchen." Nat carried three slices of pie to the table.

"I don't think so. The house rule is: if you cook for a living you can't cook dinner. Unless..." Alice set the last two plates where she and Greg had sat.

"Unless what?"

"You don't happen to specialize in desserts, do you? They might make an exception if you can bake some after-dinner sweets."

"I've dabbled in pastries and such." It wasn't her specialty or anything. She thought it might make her sound more interesting. Alice's excitement rose past a simmer and neared to a boil.

"That's it," Alice said decisively, jabbing the forks she held in Nat's direction. "Daine's got to keep you around."

"YOU CAN SAY what you want, but I think you have a great family," Nat told Daine as they walked down the front walk of his boyhood home.

"And thank goodness Greg was on his best behavior. He can make life miserable sometimes." Daine pointed out.

Even Nat could tell that Greg, with his slightly abrasive exterior, was making an effort to show his good side. A side that his wife and his mother, admittedly, said existed.

"He was trying to make a good impression for my benefit." Daine turned off his mustang's security system with a chirp. He opened the passenger door for Nat.

She flashed him a smile. Keeping his company really wasn't that bad. And it wasn't all that difficult to be nice to him. He acted more like a gentleman than the taskmaster chef she'd remembered.

His cell phone rang. "Excuse me." He stepped back from the door and pressed the phone to his ear. "Hello." A pause. "This is Daine Owens." He took a step back and moved around the front of the car.

"Natalie, are you there?" Simon called to her over the roof of the car then cupped his hands together to make a megaphone. "Come in, Natalie."

Nat swung her gaze from Daine to Simon and gave him a hardened stare.

"O-kay, so you're still with us." Simon backed off, giving Nat some breathing room. "Just wondering, we thought we might have a reception problem."

Mitch strolled toward Daine and leaned toward the phone, openly eavesdropping. "It's the police," he said. "Detective Holland."

Nat had to stand there and pretend she didn't know what was going on. But she wondered what the police wanted with Daine. How serious of a suspect was he?

"He says their preliminary tests are inconclusive and they want a blood sample to do DNA testing," Mitch repeated while Daine remained quiet.

"D. N. A?" Simon looked to Nat for an answer. "What's that?"

"He wants Daine to meet him at the Price mansion right now." Mitch sounded concerned.

"The mansion? It's the old back-to-the-scene-of-the-crime-deal," Simon said, all-knowing.

"Hang on a minute, will you?" Daine walked to the driver's side of the car. "It's the police," he said to her. "They want me to swing by the mansion right now. Do you mind?"

"Don't cross him," Simon whispered, keeping his gaze locked on *the suspect*. "You never know what a crazed killer might do."

How was Nat supposed to *act calm* after a comment like that? Besides, she was pretty sure Daine was not a killer.

"Not at all." Nat still had a hard time believing Daine was capable of murder. Sure he got angry when the kitchen's lettuce got a little wilt-y. But willing to kill the delivery boy? She didn't think so.

Daine acknowledged Nat's answer with a curt nod and went back to his phone conversation.

"They probably want to watch him for a reaction. You know, observe him at the crime scene." Simon commented with relish.

"The cops were probably swarming the joint during the funeral service." Mitch never took his eyes from Daine. "Watching everyone."

"Not everyone," Simon replied in a haughty tone. "He couldn't see us."

8

DETECTIVE HOLLAND HAD asked Nat to remain in the foyer while he and two uniformed policemen escorted Daine to the Great Room where Georgie's service had been.

"Home, sweet, home." Georgie sighed, appearing next to Nat.

"Do we have to leave? Ever? I love this house."

"Back at the scene of the crime." Mitch took off his hat and dropped it onto the large round table that held an oversized flower arrangement.

"Talk about scene of the crime...." Simon pointed at Georgie who seemed to walk single-mindedly, trance-like straight for the library.

"Oh, no. Not again," Nat murmured. That's all she needed was to get caught wandering around, especially when Detective Holland had told her to stay put.

"Go on, let's go after her." Mitch led the way, Simon followed, and Nat reluctantly moved along with them.

Nat stood at the doorway of the library and watched Georgie sit in the same spot on the leather sofa where she had before. It was the place where she'd been strangled and she reached around her neck with both hands.

Georgie's breathing deepened, grew raspier. Her eyelids fluttered shut. Every breath was a struggle.

Nat wasn't looking forward to seeing her go through the strangulation routine again. Anyone, dead or alive, choking to death wasn't pleasant to watch.

Then she stopped. The pain ebbed from Georgie's face and she straightened, her eyes widened.

"I hear it," Georgie whispered. "I can hear it."

"What? What is it?" Mitch asked. He leaned forward, interested but wary.

Nat kept quiet and looked around the room, trying to imagine what Georgie might be talking about. She didn't hear anything. Maybe it was a ghost sound.

"It's coming from back there." Georgie turned to her right, stared toward the far end of the room and pointed. "The passage. Someone's coming through the passage. I can hear the footsteps, echoing, and the door opening."

When Nat's gaze met with Mitch's she knew that they'd both seemed to remember the same thing. Georgie had told them about the secret passage the last time they were here. That's what she was talking about.

Mitch walked to the bookcase with Nat. The book that released a hidden door. Which book was it?

"Do you know which one?" Georgie had told them but Nat couldn't remember.

"Yeah. *Seven Pillars of Wisdom*, T—Something. I don't know. La— Le— Lo— L—Lawrence." Mitch pointed at a book on the third shelf from the floor.

Seven Pillars of Wisdom was a big, wide, old book, Nat stretched her hand out to push it to trigger the door as Georgie had once told her.

"Don't touch it. You'll leave fingerprints." Mitch warned. "Use something to... cover your hand."

Nat pulled off her coat and slid her hand back into her sleeve and then used her hand to push the book until she heard it *click*. She didn't bother to tell Mitch that in the twenty-first century material fibers were just as convincing evidence as fingerprints.

Nat glanced at Mitch, meeting and holding his weighted gaze while they waited for something to happen. Now what?

Nothing had happened. No passage opened, no door was even noticeable.

"No, no," Georgie moaned, then strained at the invisible threat tightening around her neck. Her voice lost its terror and she relaxed. "It's so soft. It's... it's...."

Nat moved to the sofa toward Georgie.

"Cashmere," Georgie said. "It's made out of cashmere."

"Cashmere? You were strangled with cashmere?" Simon sounded aghast. "A scarf?"

"I can smell... I smell..." Georgie continued, working to get the words out.

"You don't anymore, blondie. Remember, you're history." Mitch scolded her, sounding impatient. Simon shushed him and kept his full attention on Georgie.

Nat stood riveted, hanging on Georgie's every word, waiting for her to say the next.

"Ninja." Georgie mouthed and repeated it much softer than a whisper. "*Nin-ja*."

"Here you are," Daine said with a mild surprise of discovery. He stopped at the library door and glanced around, perhaps wondering what she was doing there, seemingly alone. He didn't seem upset after his meeting with the police.

In the drama of Georgie's declaration of Ninja— the cologne,

Nat, as the other three near her, froze. They, unlike Nat, disappeared into thin air at Daine's arrival.

"They've finished with me. We can go," he said.

At that moment Nat wanted nothing more than to leave the room and get out of that house. The creep factor was really getting to her. Just as she took her first step, a loud, odd creak came from across the room.

"What's that?" Daine took a few steps past Nat, nearing the wall of bookcases where she thought the sound had come. Part of the case had swung open to reveal a passage.

"Hold it, right there." The man's voice came from the doorway.

Nat didn't move a muscle. Daine did the same. Detective Holland stalked into the room and motioned for them to step aside.

"How did this get here?" he asked.

Nat and Daine looked at one another and if one could shrug in a glance, that's what they did.

"Did you know about this?" Holland walked cautiously to the passage and peered inside. He pulled a pen from his pocket and used it to flip on a light switch on the right. He took another look, this time much longer.

"Where did that come from?" Daine asked no one in particular and Nat preferred to regard the question as a rhetorical one.

The detective straightened and turned back toward them. "You two have a seat over there." He indicated that they should sit on the murder-sofa.

Daine, who must have been much braver than Nat, sat in the middle. Nat, who knew where Georgie had been *done in*, sat on the other side, to the left of Daine.

Holland pulled out his phone and punched a button. "Yeah, don't pack up shop just yet, come in the library. I want you to dust for more prints."

Daine turned to look at Nat and she thought that he must be thinking the same thing—prints? They must already have Daine's. Whose then? Hers?

"I'm sorry Nat," he said, his voice laden with guilt-ridden sympathy.

Holland pocketed his phone and headed around the sofa to face them, but he stared at her. He pulled out a small spiral-bound notebook and his pen. "What's your connection with Mr. Owens, here."

Nat opened her mouth to say something and found her voice missing, her mouth dry. She cleared her throat and tried to swallow before answering. "We're friends." She glanced at Daine, making sure it was all right to call their rekindled acquaintance that. "And former colleagues."

"So you work in the kitchen, too?"

Another quick peek at Daine told her that the *kitchen work* description might mean she packed orders from a fast food joint and not someone who trained and practiced skills from the culinary arts.

"Could I get your name, for the record?"

For the record sounded serious, so cop-like like she might have had something to do with the murder. Did this mean he was including her in his investigation?

Nat didn't know anything, except what Georgie had told her. She couldn't tell Detective Holland that because she'd sound like a crazy person for saying she could talk to dead people. Then he might have to have her locked up at the funny farm or at least have her dragged away by men in white coats for observation. Whatever... this wasn't looking good.

Holland was still staring at her, waiting.

"I'm sorry what did you want?" Nat blinked.

"Your name?" he repeated.

Oh, yeah, she remembered. *For the record.*

"My name is Natalie Powell."

He scribbled it down in his notebook. Then he asked where she lived, her phone number, and where she worked. He wrote all of that down, too. Then he asked how well and how long had she known the deceased.

Nat remembered the story she and Georgie had made up, the same one she told Daine, the big lie she'd told everyone that would be now *on the record*.

"All right, you two, can you tell me what you know about this passage, over there." Holland looked from one to the other.

"Nothing," Daine said, which convinced Nat.

"Nothing," Nat said, which was another lie. But she hadn't known about it ten minutes ago even though she'd been the one to open it. But she wasn't going to mention that.

The two very serious-looking men Nat had seen when she first arrived were back with another two men, carrying what looked like a mismatched set of luggage.

"I'd like to have Miss Powell's fingerprints taken" —Holland turned to Nat— "if that's all right with you?"

"No problem," Nat replied. Like declining wouldn't make her look guilty. What else could she say?

She understood why the police wanted her fingerprints and she was glad she'd followed Mitch's suggestion and had not touched the book that released the door.

"Get some shots of that," Holland ordered the crew. "And I want the whole tamale dusted for prints." He turned to Nat and Daine. "It might be a good idea not to plan any trips." He winked. "You know the routine, you need to stick around. Someplace where we can get a hold of you if we need to."

He might think she was going to make a break for it. But Nat hadn't done anything wrong. Well, almost nothing. She had, after all, opened the door to the secret passage. If Georgie was right and the murderer had come through the passage, then Nat opening the secret door might help find the killer.

———

DAINE PULLED UP in front of Nat's apartment building. "Do you mind if I walk you in?"

The ride home felt pretty tense. Nat got a taste of the pressure he felt. Except in his case, he might actually be guilty.

"Sure. Come on up." They got out of the car and he followed her upstairs. Nat unlocked the door, took three quick steps down the short, dark hall, and flipped on the dim hallway light. If the light had already been on, Nat would have known Becca was home. Since it was off, she knew that she and Daine were alone.

He followed her in and hovered next to the front door while Nat bent into the kitchen and hit the switch for the fluorescent light. Nothing happened.

"Oh, that stupid kitchen light." Nat shrugged at their surroundings. "Sorry, do you want to come in and sit for a while? Have a cup of coffee?"

"No, I don't want you to go to any trouble. I just wanted to say how much I appreciate what you've done."

Without the bright kitchen light, the mood in the hallway might have been almost romantic. That's if she were standing here with someone else other than Daine.

But romance with Daine was the farthest thing from her mind. "What did I do?" Nat was fairly sure he didn't know anything about her part in the discovery.

"You let me subject you to my family. For that, I owe you big time." Now she knew why Daine was here. He wanted to express his gratitude.

Nat glanced around to make sure their moment was private. No signs of any obvious unwanted observers.

Like Mitch, Simon, or Georgie.

"I didn't think I'd have to drag you to a meeting with the police or have them imply that you're involved in Georgette's death. I'm really sorry."

"What can I say? I was in the wrong place at the wrong time." Nat wanted to change the subject, fast. "I'm not worried about it. I'm not involved."

"Well, if there's anything I can do for you...." He held out a business card with two fingers. "You can give me a call anytime."

"How about that job at Sam's?" she suggested, only half-joking. Why not.

"I've already made my recommendation, the owners haven't made up their minds yet. If it were up to me—" Daine smiled. "I'd love to have you under me." His eyes shot open and the smile left his lips. He must have been horrified by what he said. "I mean— that's not what I meant."

He sounded embarrassed. Nat thought that if he hadn't had that goatee or if the lighting had been brighter she might have even seen him blush.

"It's all right. I know what you mean," she said, trying to put him at ease.

Working under him, there was something she did not want to think about.

"Well, despite the last stop I wanted to tell you that I'm glad I had the chance to spend time with you. I really enjoy your company."

"Me, too," she said more out of politeness than pure truth. Was telling half-lies better than full-blown ones?

"I hope we can see each other again." Daine moved toward Nat, slowly. "We don't have to have an excuse, do we?"

"No, we don't." She could tell that he was going to kiss her. Nat wasn't sure she wanted that but something inside her told her to let him.

Okay, okay, she'd would. Was this some sort of unconscious strategy on her part or was there something else? Curiosity?

He leaned closer. Nat could feel the heat from his body as he neared. She closed her eyes not to prepare for the kiss but so she didn't have to see him that close up. Nat braced herself and felt the slightest brush of his lips to hers. The clattering of metal hitting porcelain clattered from the hallway. It shattered the moment and she stepped back.

"What was that?"

"I'm sure it's nothing." But in her mind's eye, Nat could picture the car fob in its bowl in the kitchen by the phone and knew that's what made the sound.

All by themselves?

Probably not. They probably had some other-world help.

There was an awkward, quiet moment that followed while they were standing there, not sure of what they should do. It was clear that they were not going to repeat the kiss.

"I guess I'll say goodnight." Nat walked him to the front door and latched it close behind him. To assure she would remain alone, she threw the deadbolt.

MITCH WATCHED NATALIE return to the kitchen. He leaned against the counter, bending the brim of his hat before he pulled it off. Well within reach of the keyring that sat in the blue and white porcelain bowl, he glanced up at her and shrugged.

He couldn't do much, but he did what he could do. And it seemed to do the trick. She was here and the jerk had left. And that's exactly what he wanted.

"Watch it, *doll*," Mitch finally said, then dropped his Trilby on the counter. "That guy's thinking he's roped you and all he needs to do is pull you in. I can tell by the way he watches you."

Natalie said nothing, just stared at him.

"He thinks you're on his side. You're there for him and you're gonna come running when he calls for you. That's what he's thinking, anyway." Mitch knew all about ulterior motives. He'd had plenty of them during his time. He pushed off the counter and strolled over to her. "I wouldn't trust that Joe as far as I could throw him."

Maybe Simon was right. Maybe Mitch did have a touch of the green-eyed monster lurking in him. Mitch couldn't stand the sight of Daine.

He could admit it to himself. But never to Simon, who would make the biggest fuss about it and come up with a dozen possible reasons why, and worst of all, take every opportunity to razz him. Mitch didn't need to listen to that.

It was more than keeping Natalie away from a possible murderer. Mitch wanted her away from that burger jockey because he was a flesh-and-blood man. And there was no way Mitch could ever compete with that.

Natalie marched up to him and he straightened, standing just as close to her as Daine had. Mitch glanced from her lips to her eyes, measuring the interest she held for him. If he were not mistaken, her heartbeat had doubled.

"What does he think he's doing talking about cops and jobs?" He kept his voice soft and low. She had to stay near him to hear him. "That's no way to talk to a lady."

By the rise and fall of her chest, he could tell her breathing had tripled. Her face softened, she'd parted her lips to breathe. She inhaled deeper. Mitch had that effect on women, always had.

"What we need with this soft lighting is a whine of a muted trombone." He recalled the exact sound. Natalie's gaze darted from side to side as if trying to find the source of the music he had created for her. "A warm breeze blowing by while Dinah Shore sings For Sentimental Reasons."

A gentle breeze swept by, at the mention of the song, ruffling her hair and all trace tension in her face melted away. His memory of Dinah's mellow voice filled the room. Mitch shifted his weight from one foot to the other in time to the music. Natalie swayed, mirroring him, staring into his eyes in a hypnotic fashion.

She heard it, too. He made her hear it.

He held his hand out, as if to take hers, and curled his other arm around her waist. She raised her hand to rest in his, but of course, she couldn't touch him. Although he might have looked solid to her, Mitch had no substance.

She swallowed and took a deep breath.

Natalie looked so beautiful, enticing. Her hourglass curves convinced him to give the chance of hugging them a shot. How he wanted this to be real. How he wished... How he wanted... He tightened his arm around her waist... but it wasn't possible.

The overhead lights in the kitchen flickered on, flooding the hallway with bright light.

"Did you say Din-o-saur?" Georgie's high-pitched voice filled the air. "Is that like a band from your time or something?"

Mitch took a step back when he'd realized they weren't alone.

"No, it's Dinah *Shore*," Simon clarified, appearing next to Georgie. "She's a singer who has a talk show and shame on her, she's robbed the cradle. Her new boyfriend is some new young buck actor—Burt Reynolds."

NAT WOKE BLEARY-EYED and checked the clock on her nightstand. 4:27 a.m. She'd been asleep for just over an hour. What woke her?

"Well, it meant something." One voice insisted—a man's. "We didn't even have time to talk about this, she just went straight off to bed."

"Just because she's not willing to discuss it doesn't mean that we can't go on without her," a second voice said—a second man's.

"I don't think she should have anything more to do with that over-blown short order cook. That guy's trouble." There was no mistaking Mitch's growl, even from another room.

"She has to keep seeing him. He's important, he could be the killer. How else are we going to find out?"

"That's exactly why Natalie doesn't need to be hanging around him. The cops are gonna be on to him soon. Doesn't tonight prove it?"

"I think I see the green-eyed monster peeking out again." That was Simon.

"You know what? You're nuts," came the accusation from Mitch.

And that wasn't the end of it. Simon said something then Mitch snapped back. Over and over and over again, they wouldn't give it a rest.

"Oh, for goodness' sake." Nat threw back her covers and marched out of her bedroom into the living room. She gave her cotton boxers a hike after a few steps. "Why? Why do you have to argue in the middle of the night so everyone can hear you?"

Georgie, Simon, and Mitch stared at Nat. Nat looked down at her sleep rumpled *Sweet Dreams* sleep shirt.

"You know, I think I used to have some skivvies exactly like that." Mitch pointed at Nat's boxers.

"*Everyone* can't hear us, but they can hear you yelling at us." Georgie pointed out with an innocent blink.

Even this early in the morning Nat knew that. "Great, so I'm the only person who's awakened at four-thirty in the morning."

"If you don't keep your voice down, you'll wake the neighbors." Simon pressed his index finger to his lips and with a jerk of his head indicated the walls. "Paper thin, you know."

Nat gave an exasperated sigh. "Can't you talk someplace else?"

"Not really, the only place we can *talk* is when we're here," Simon told her.

"In my living room?" Nat noticed both Mitch's hat and Georgie's purse on her coffee table.

"Not specifically," Simon clarified. "And we'd like to include you in our discussion."

"Wonderful." Nat gave up. She wasn't going to get rid of them and she wasn't going to get any more sleep.

"It's part of the rules." Mitch finished. "We have to be near you."

"You didn't even tell us what went on in my father's library yesterday." Georgie made it sound as if Nat had been keeping it from them on purpose.

"You're the ones who left." Nat sunk onto the sofa and tucked her legs under her. "Did you hear what that Detective Holland said to me? He made it sound like I might be involved with the murder."

"What did you tell him?" Georgie might have thought she sounded casual but the tone of her question implied anything but. She wanted answers.

"No, I... I used the *personal chef* story. The same one I told Skinner and your two girlfriends."

"Liz and Dahlia," Georgie said their names, half in reminiscence and half as if to remind herself that she could remember them.

"Good," Mitch agreed. "I find that it's best to keep your lies straight."

That sounded like advice from a person who knew first hand. Somehow Nat didn't find it difficult to imagine that Mitch had lots of practice and was adept at bending the truth.

"The police found the passageway. They're checking it for fingerprints but they aren't going to find mine." Nat hadn't stepped one foot inside.

"It'll be interesting to see who they come up with." Mitch sounded ever-so patient.

"They're going to be wrong," Georgie said with full confidence.

"How do you know?" If these three could see into the future, that would be news. Nat didn't think so. One of them might have mentioned having the ability of foresight sometime before this.

"The scarf," Georgie began. "The cashmere scarf that— it's my father's—was my father's. I smelled the Ninja cologne. He always wore it."

Georgie had made the leap from her first impressions of the murder weapon, the feel, the smell of it, linking it to its owner. That's what was important enough to wake Nat, that's what they wanted to tell her. In this case, the scarf's owner could not have been the murderer. Could he?

"But your father died more than six months ago." Nat made what she thought was the connection. "No way. That can't have happened." She looked to Simon then Mitch for a confirmation or denial.

"Dead people can't kill the living," Simon stated, making it crystal clear.

"Is that a rule, too?" Nat asked Mitch.

"I don't know if it's a rule but I think it's pretty much impossible." So Mitch didn't know everything, nor could he lend any insight on the subject.

"Can you check?" Nat motioned into the cosmos. "Somewhere... out there?"

"We don't have Western Union out here, sister." Mitch stared at Nat in a way that made her feel uncomfortable but not in a dead-guy-looking-at-her kind. Although that might give anyone the creeps.

But they, or at least Mitch, had some unusual talents, some ability to affect the living world. She thought back to a few hours earlier when he did that weird thing that made her hear music, made her go into some kind of weird trance. It made her shiver. Who knew what else he was capable of?

"So what, the cops find out that the scarf belongs to Daddy-dear?" Simon was playing devil's advocate. "What does that mean? They can't pin it on him, he's on our side, now."

"Yeah, well, they'll find out who had that scarf." Mitch looked to Georgie for an answer. "Do you know?"

"No." But it was clear by the expression on her face that she was deep in thought, working on it.

"What will the police discover when they look at your father's scarf?" Nat wished she could put herself in that position and imagine, but a lab technician was as far away from food prep as you could get. "Daine said the police wanted another sample. I think they needed a sample of his blood because their preliminary DNA tests were inconclusive."

"What is D-N-A?" Simon turned to Nat for an answer. There was no way he or Mitch could know what it was.

"Scientists have ways of finding genetic markers found in blood or hair now. If they can match the markers, they can tell if two pieces of DNA come from the same person." Nat did her best to make it understandable. "I think it has to do with blood type and genetics. Maybe they're getting Mr. Price's DNA from his scarf and it's a partial match to Daine or Greg's and it's throwing them off."

"Maybe it is and maybe it isn't." Mitch shrugged. "You still don't know who could have gotten their hands on the scarf. Not only is it possible, it's probable."

Mitch looked at her in the strangest way. Almost as if he were angry with her. What was his problem?

9

MITCH CLOSED HIS eyes and squeezed them as hard as he could. He could not stop thinking about it. It was driving him crazy. He could not, would not stand there and watch her kiss *that* man. But in his mind, he saw them together.

Daine.

It made Mitch's blood boil. A woman shouldn't just kiss a man, a man whom she has no feeling for, whom she does not love. And she did not love him. He knew that much.

In an instant, every woman who'd kissed him, given their bodies so willingly to him, flashed through his mind. He hadn't loved them. And most of them hadn't loved him. But they'd all done it, kissed him—willingly. He'd kissed them back, taken what they had to offer without a second thought.

Most of them hadn't loved him. But some had. And now he regretted it. The thought of breaking their hearts made him hurt inside.

But that was impossible. He couldn't feel. Shouldn't be able to. He must be imagining it; the ache, the heaviness, the pain.

The stark white of his surroundings faded to gray and then he neither saw nor sensed anything around him.

Now he knew. He'd thought that all those women he had bedded felt nothing, as he had, they were taking a tumble in the sack for a bit of fun, that's all.

But he knew better. There were a few women, maybe more than a few, who had thought their fling was more than that.

Only now did he realize that their meaningless sex hadn't been quite that for some of them. Now he knew he'd been wrong. He'd hurt them. It hadn't been merely meaningless on his part, it had been *thoughtless*.

Hearts could be broken. Theirs, not his.

He'd never believed in love but now, because of Natalie, he knew better. Mitch knew it now because his heart was breaking. He placed his hands over his chest and pressed hard. He wanted it to stop.

His legs went weak and buckled. He dropped onto his knees and collapsed forward, resting his forearms on the floor.

Never, ever again, he swore. He would never make a commitment to the flesh without love first. *Sin* seemed to be the only way to explain what he'd done. It was unforgivable. Yet he had not burned in hell, he was here.

Women always talked of 'being in love' and Mitch had thought it was only a silly female notion. Songs of love boasted of abounding happiness and a feeling of soaring, he felt none of this. Okay, he was in love and now he could admit it, but the timing was wrong.

If... When... he had it to do all over again, he'd promised, vowed to himself that he would do it right. He would never share his life, *himself* with anyone unless he were in love. Completely in love, as he was with Natalie.

The realization that he was in love with her made him sad. He had never been in love, never thought such a thing existed. He'd never known anyone like her.

She couldn't have an inkling of what he felt for her. He only just realized it and he would never confess to anyone how much he cared, loved, and admired her. The most upsetting of all was that he could never tell Natalie. Because he was here and she was... out there, on the other side.

He was in love alone.

It felt horrible. Now he got it. He understood. He'd hurt so many people, broken marriages and probably far worse. Being shot dead had been too good for him. He should have died a more painful death. He deserved it.

Well, payback's a bitch and now he suffered. The ache in his chest felt all too real and it was doing its job by splitting him in half.

Fine. Let him suffer. Mitch pushed himself upright and struggled to get to his feet. The thought that he couldn't have her—ever —sustained his pain.

It didn't matter. He didn't matter. She was after a murderer. The only thing that mattered was to keep her safe.

He felt haunted by the many women he had used and tossed aside. He was so sorry. Sorrier than he could ever say. It was too late to make amends to them.

Tears leaked from his eyes and ran down his cheeks. The unwanted, heavy feeling pulsing through him was real. Now he knew that love and caring more for someone else than for one's self was possible.

He knew. He understood. He felt it.

If there were only a way to fix things, make amends. He would do it.

In a heartbeat.

What Mitch needed was a second chance.

10

***

DID NAT HAVE to wake up *every* morning to the ghostly grumbles?

"How long do we have to wait?" Georgie's shrill and impatient voice carried right through the wall into Nat's bedroom. "*That* might be important."

Nat didn't know what *that* Georgie was referring to, but until she got out of bed and went to see for herself the non-stop tirade wasn't going to end, of that she was sure.

"It's not up to us. We can only do so much or go so far on our own." Simon sounded much calmer but not any happier. "We have our limitations."

"It's taken forever to get the tiniest lead and now that we have something—" Was that Georgie pounding things and stomping around? "Something that could be vitally important—*she's* got to snooze the morning away and—"

Nat couldn't help from hearing them. Didn't they know that she needed sleep? She threw her covers back, slid out of bed, and smoothed her nightshirt before marching to the door and wrenching it open.

"Do you think you can keep it down out here?" she shouted at them.

"Sorry, Nat." Becca froze with her tall, stainless commuter cup in hand.

Nat's gaze moved from Simon and Georgie and locked on to Becca who wasn't the noisy one.

"Hurry, come see this." Georgie waved her over and pointed to a small sheet of paper lying on the counter. "You've got to call her back right away."

"Sorry. I guess I'm a little grouchy." Becca looked truly apologetic that she'd disturbed her sister, but it hadn't been her fault. "You want some coffee?"

"Sure." She took a breath, swiped at the tell-tale sleepiness from around her eyes, and rubbed her neck. "Is this for me?" Nat glanced at the note: *Call Dahlia. 1-650-555-5499*

"Yeah, she called last night." Becca filled the coffee cup.

"Wait a minute." Nat worked real hard at putting the pieces of what she saw together. "You're making your own coffee. You usually go to... What's going on? What's going on with Theo? Things are still okay with you two, right?"

"Forget about Theo." Georgie huffed in exasperation. "You have to return Dahlia's call. It might be something really important."

"He thought it might be a good idea if we had a little time apart." The tightness in her voice and the forced calm told Nat that Becca didn't share that thought.

"Give her a sec, Georgie," Simon said to her in a way that was bossy yet not pushy in its delivery. "Why don't you sit down next to me and we'll wait together."

Nat ignored Georgie's head shaking and huffing, continuing her focus on Becca. "You think you might have been rushing things?" It was a question she asked with each of Becca's boyfriends.

"I thought he felt the same way I did." Becca sniffed and it wasn't long before a tear, then two, followed, trailing down her cheek.

"No man feels commitment unless you spell it with a dollar sign." Georgie sounded like she was talking from experience. "And a lot of zeros."

"Maybe you just misread him." Nat felt it difficult to sympathize with her sister. It had been only four months since the last time this had happened.

"He said that things were moving too fast for him. That's all." Becca swiped at her face and pushed Nat's coffee cup toward her across the counter.

"That's the fifty-first way to leave your lover," Simon said. "Used that 'moving too fast' excuse myself more times than I've had it used on me. He probably won't give her the time of day because she's already shacked up with him."

"What about you?" Becca spun the questioning back at Nat. "You heard from Daine yet? How did your first date go? Did you two—"

"It was fine," Nat replied. "And nothing happened between us."

"He hasn't called you, has he?" Becca's expression told it all. Nat's "date" had been a failure. Daine would never call Nat to see her again.

"I... well." Nat hadn't really thought of that night as bad. She hadn't gone with him because she liked him, she needed to because..... "It doesn't matter."

"He probably wouldn't have called if she'd slept with him. But she hadn't so why hasn't he called?" Simon glanced at Nat, letting his gaze linger. "On second thought, I'm not so sure he was even thinking of moving in that direction. Unless he thinks you're playing hard to get and he's a man who doesn't play games he might not even know the rules in which case he's clueless anyway."

"I'm not worried about him," Nat said casually but shot Simon a hardened look. Being dead wasn't going to save him. "I need to call Dahlia."

"Who's that? I've never heard her name before."

"I met her at the funeral, too."

Becca's arm froze, her coffee cup halfway to her lips. "Is this a new trend for you? Meeting people at funerals? That's really gross, Nat."

"Dahlia was... nice." Nat tried to think of something truthful and believable to say.

"Are you kidding? Dahlia's the best." Georgie added.

"Is she into cooking?"

"We talked about food," Nat said, trying to remember their conversation. "And... purses."

"Purses?" Becca didn't just stare at Nat she gawked. "You?"

"I have a purse. I—"

"What you have isn't a purse. It's more like a cross body tote."

Nat's bag, okay, tote that she used as a carry-all worked just fine. Just because she didn't have a dozen filling her closet didn't mean she was any less of a woman.

"Aren't you going to be late for work or something?" Nat couldn't wait for her sister to leave. If Becca stuck around any longer they were going to have one of their major sibling squabbles. It happened about every other year and they were due for a major blow-up. Nat didn't want to do it with an audience.

"I'm off to work, then." Becca checked the lid on her travel mug and left.

"Call her now." Georgie urged Nat when the front door closed. "It could be really important. Find out what she wants."

There would be no peace until Georgie got her way. Nat grabbed the kitchen wall phone and punched in Dahlia's number.

"Hello?" Georgie perceptively melted when she heard her friend's voice.

"Hi, Dahlia, this is Natalie Powell."

"Nat! I'm so glad you called back. Liz and I need someone else who can help us decide what to do."

"About what?"

"About Georgie's charity auction." She said it as if it were common knowledge. "*Everybody* knows we're doing it."

Nat stared at Georgie who stood sagging against the counter. "An auction... in... my memory?"

"How touching," Nat said, seeing for herself that it had pleased Georgie. "I know she would have loved the idea."

"Yes, it's for her favorite charity."

"The Children's Hospital." Georgie sobbed.

"The Children's Hospital?" Nat repeated.

"That's right. I guess it isn't a surprise to you that she felt as if she had to do something or those less fortunate than her."

"That sounds" —Nat gulped and smiled at Georgie— "just like her."

"You know, it's the way she was..." Dahlia went on. And on, and on. Georgie punctuated the pauses with small selfless remarks and sobs.

Nat sipped her coffee and waited for it all to be over and hoped Dahlia would get to the point soon.

"You've just got to help us," Dahlia finally said. "Liz and I can't agree on anything and we don't want to ask anyone else in our group. They're only casual friends and acquaintances. We need an impartial third party, but not just anyone. We need someone who *really* knows her."

Was that Nat's cue to say something?

"Oh, yes," Georgie sniffed. "You have to help them, Natalie. They *need* you."

Nat wasn't so sure about how much she was needed or what she could do for them but agreed. Dahlia and Georgie both cheered while Simon stuck his fingers in his ears, pretending he didn't hear a word.

"I'm going to call and tell Liz. Meet us at Georgie's house in two hours."

TWO HOURS LATER, Nat showed up at the Price Mansion. Skinner opened the front door and greeted her. Liz and Dahlia squealed a welcome from the second story landing. Again Georgie sobbed at the sight of her friends.

"I'm so glad you're here," Liz exclaimed, linking her arm through Nat's on the right side. "We've gone through her first three closets and sorted them into different piles."

The first *three*? How many more closets did that leave, exactly?

"We've got a huge number of items for the auction," Dahlia told Nat. "There are a few things that need to be returned to the designers. They asked to have their pieces returned, not given away. Then we have some dresses and accessories for donations."

"Did you know that *they* were going to throw all her clothes and bags away?" Liz huffed in outrage.

"*They* who?" Nat turned to Liz.

"The lawyers," she said in a low and spite-filled tone that let Nat know exactly what she'd thought of Georgie's legal beagles.

"Liz and I know how precious Georgie's wardrobe was to her. They didn't dare object to us having the auction and sending the proceeds to charity as long as it was done in her name." Dahlia certainly sounded driven as she and Liz took charge of this effort for such a worthy cause.

"It's the least we can do for her." Liz started getting weepy.

"Oh, you guys are so sweet," Georgie sobbed into her handkerchief.

"I think this would have really meant a lot to Georgie." Nat was only telling the truth.

"If I can't bring it with me, someone should enjoy it all." Georgie managed to whisper.

"She already has the entire winter Nicole Madison Collection. It's not even out yet."

Georgie sobbed louder.

It would seem that being dead wasn't half as bad as not being able to wear the new designer collection.

"Whoever buys it has to be a size 2, though." Liz pointed out.

None of the clothing would come close to fitting Nat.

"And even more importantly, wear a size 4 shoe," Dahlia added.

Ditto. Nat's honkin' size 7s were not going to fit either.

"Her bag collection is awesome. They'll make hundreds of people very happy." Liz smiled and blotted her nose.

They spent the next four hours in Georgie's humongous spring closet. It seemed crowded with five of them there. Only Liz and Dahlia could see three people and they told Nat the background story and possible future plans for every item of clothing, pairs of shoes, and each accessory.

Georgie was very emotional and Simon did his best to comfort her. Both of them were fascinated, Nat was bored stiff, and Mitch must have had the good sense not to show up.

Then out came a purse. Not a purse, it was a bag, no it was more of a sack. No, what it really looked like a giant fig. A giant fig with a bunch of gold-colored chains hanging around it.

"My dumpling!" Georgie cried out. "You found Dumpling! I thought I'd lost it!"

"It's her favorite bag!" Liz hugged the bag tight. "It's been missing for months."

"*Dumpling?*" Nat hated to utter the words.

"That's exactly what she used to call it." Dahlia touched the bag with the utmost reverence.

Nat didn't want to get near it.

"It's big, but not too big." Georgie held it up to show its size. "And it's got all these dividers and tons of pockets to put stuff in. And a special compartment for your cell phone and keys. In the bottom," she said from behind her handkerchief. "I have a secret pocket on the bottom. That's where I keep my emergency platinum card. Just in case."

In case of what? Nat couldn't help but take a long side-glance at Georgie. The idea was ridiculous since she probably had a ten ga-zillion dollar limit, even she had to have a problem hitting that.

"Someone is going to be very lucky when they get this." Liz admired the bag. "It's the best purse ever."

NAT STEPPED INSIDE her apartment, closed, and leaned back against the door. "Where's Mitch?" She was going to give him an earful. How could he leave her alone with *them*? She needed *him* there, needed someone to sympathize with her. She wanted someone to feel sorry for her for enduring *that*, all of that... talk.

And he would. She knew how much he hated all that girly stuff.

"I'm not sure where he is." Simon who had appeared, sitting on the sofa, glanced around only now realizing his absence. "I think he's gone."

"What do you mean *gone*?" Nat set her purse and the car fob on the kitchen counter.

"*Gone* as in not here. Come to think of it," Simon said with a thoughtful finger placed on his cheek. "I haven't seen him for quite a while."

"He's someplace, isn't he?" A sense of panic came over Nat.

No Mitch? He was always around *someplace*. "Georgie, have you seen Mitch?"

Georgie's gaze darted around the room. "I don't think so, but he doesn't matter." She dismissed the subject of him with a wave of her hand. "I've just remembered something."

Nat stared at Georgie, waiting for the news.

"When daddy died, I sent some of his things to Greg and Daine. I thought they might want something of his. He was their father, too."

Wasn't she the considerate one? Georgie must not have known that it had been years since her brothers had any contact from their father.

"I sent each of them one of his overcoats, two of his nicest suits, and six scarves," Georgie listed. "I sent them six each because he had twelve. When they got worn he'd replace them, but he always had twelve."

Nat knew where Georgie was leading. "So if there's a way we can see, count how many Greg and Daine each have—"

"If either of them is missing one of the six...." Simon began, catching up to the thought wave.

"Exactly." Georgie locked gazes with Nat then Simon. All three knew the next step.

"Daine should be easy if you can ever get a hold of him. Getting inside Greg's house might be more of a problem." In Mitch's absence, Simon stepped in to mastermind the plan of attack.

"That's even if they still have them." Nat could see that even if she managed to do an in-house scarf check there could be problems. "They could have been already donated to some used-clothing store."

"We have to try." Simon encouraged Nat. "It's the only lead we've got."

"All you have to do is get inside the house. Once you're there, even if it's only for a few minutes, we can do the rest." Simon assured Nat and with a curt nod, he promised Georgie they'd do this.

Georgie pointed at the phone, lying on the counter. "Come on, Natalie, let's go."

Another inside peek at Georgie's life was important but what about Mitch? She missed that cool, skeptical look he used to give her—the cleft in his chin, that out-of-style, weird suit he wore, and that dumb hat.

"Call him," Georgie ordered. "Call him now."

"Call him and say what?"

Simon shrugged. "You'll think of something."

Nat lifted the phone and dialed. The phone rang only once before Daine picked up.

"It's Natalie," she said. "Natalie Powell."

"I was just going to call you." Daine's words came out in a rush as if he were genuinely excited to talk to her.

"Really?" Did he say that because he meant it or had it said that just to be polite? Nat couldn't imagine why he'd want to call her. "What's going on?"

"It's nothing important really. It's just... this is short notice so I'd understand if you're unavailable. I just got the call about an hour ago and you were the first person I thought of for—" He began but he didn't sound like he didn't care if she said no. "I was wondering if you'd be interested in—I need an assistant for a cooking segment for Evening Magazine."

Evening Magazine... the TV show?

"The theme is *Summer Barbecue in an Hour—Six Dishes in Sixty Minutes.*"

Nat hadn't expected this. She was thinking he might want to go out for coffee, maybe dinner. But to appear on a local television show....

"It's mostly prep work. We'll have to precook the menu for final display and to show a few in-between stages."

"Do it. Do it." Georgie and Simon chanted together and not particularly in sync. "Say yes." They moved closer, crowding her.

Nat turned away from them, hoping for a bit of privacy she was sure she wouldn't get.

"So are you interested? It would make a nice bullet on your résumé," Daine tempted.

"It's the perfect excuse to see him," Georgie said to Simon, happy that Nat's culinary opportunity was also a chance to bring them together.

"I'm sure that even you can find an excuse to go back to his place." Simon voiced some doubt whether Nat could manage it. "Maybe there you could manage to find something incriminating about him. He might slip up, say something to give himself away."

Playing super-sleuth was not Nat's strongpoint but she was thinking it over. She must have eventually said yes to Daine because he was giving her the details of where they had to go, what time they had to be there, and when he'd be picking her up tomorrow morning. She had been only half-listening, this was one time she didn't mind Georgie and Simon eavesdropping because they filled her in on what she'd missed.

"What did you want?" Daine fell silent so Nat could answer. "You're the one who called me, remember?"

"Oh, yeah." Nat had been side-tracked, she'd lost her *Get Daine* momentum, and she had no idea what she was going to say.

"Greg," Georgie reminded her. "You have to go to Greg's house, check how many scarves he has."

"Your brother, Greg." Nat cleared her throat, buying herself a few seconds. "I mean, his wife, Alice." She paused again, for another couple of seconds. "We were talking about desserts and pastries and she seemed really interested when I told her that I dabbled in baking. Well, I thought I'd give her a call and see if I could drop off some of the... pieces I baked. I wonder if you could give me her number?"

"You're baking today?" Daine's voice sounded soft and breathless.

"I like to bake on my days off," she said bravely, but rather stilted. She did like to bake but rarely had the time to indulge.

"What did you bake?"

"Choc-co... late..." Nat said the first thing that came to mind then she had to finish her answer. "...um... éclairs."

"Cream or custard?"

"Um... both." She should have just kept her mouth shut. What the heck was she thinking? *Both*. Nat rolled her eyes. *Stoopid*.

"My favorite," Daine whispered back.

"Which?" Nat could have sworn she heard his mouth water over the line.

"*Both*," he murmured. "Greg'll divorce Alice if he finds out she turned down éclairs."

Alice wasn't kidding about the two brothers liking their desserts. Nat would have never thought an iced brownie or any other kind of simple home-baked confection might be the key to getting into their house.

"Now you got him," Simon cheered. "You've got him eating out of the palm of your hand."

"They live in Hillsborough. Alice gets home around three." Daine gave Nat his sister-in-law's cell number.

"And you? Would you like me to drop off an éclair or two? From one hard-working chef to another?" Nat glanced at Daine's business card and noticed his address. He lived across the San Francisco bay from his brother. "I can swing by later if you'd like."

"Sure. Thanks." Something in Daine's voice changed. "That's really nice of you."

"No problem. Just want to share the goodness."

"Great, I'm looking forward to it." A shuffle of papers filled the momentary silence. "I'm still planning the menu, I've got to get back to those people and let them know."

"You get back to work, then. I'll see you in a few hours." Nat hung up.

"You're not working today?" Simon asked Nat in disbelief. "Since when?"

Nat closed her eyes and pressed her hand to her forehead. "I don't know why I said that." That was an out and out lie. She did not have the day off.

"It doesn't matter. Don't go. Call in sick." Georgie shrugged.

"I can't just skip work." Nat had the horrible feeling this wasn't the end of it. Only the latest in her already long line of lies she'd already told.

"It's only a job." Georgie sassed and had no idea what Nat had to do to get to this position. "We might be here forever but that doesn't mean I want to spend eternity with you."

Nat swung around and sent a less than pleased look her way. "You're not the life of the party, either."

Simon sliced through the icy silence that followed. "So, how long does it take to make a batch of éclairs?" He glanced at the clock on the microwave. "It's nearly ten now."

"Considering I have no ingredients and almost none of the tools I'll need, that'll mean shopping." Nat snatched up a pen and pulled over a pad of paper to make a list. "I need to make choux pastry. I'll need flour, eggs, milk, butter— I don't have near enough at home. Then there are the custard and cream fillings," she mumbled, going through the ingredients she'd need.

"No way." Georgie was losing patience with Nat and walked away from her. "Just go to Tout Sweets and buy them there."

"Buy them?" Nat's pen slipped from her hand and clattered onto the counter. "I can't do that."

"Why not? You're the one who said it would take forever. You can't make them. What choice do you have?" Georgie was less than pleasant. "This isn't the Great American Éclair Contest, you're not being judged in some World Class taste test. You need to get those éclairs and get moving."

Georgie was right. There wasn't time to do anything else. Nat was going to spend the rest of the day driving around the bay area playing a delivery boy. Her first stop would be Tout Sweets for éclairs.

They would look good, taste delicious, and probably impress everyone, even though she hadn't made them herself. Hopefully, she wouldn't get caught passing them off as her own.

"Come on, Natalie, we've got to get going." Simon was sounding more and more like Georgie. Whiney.

"All right. I'll do it. Just give me a minute." Nat gave in, hoping Simon would stop. "First things first. Before I call Alice, I've got to call into work."

Nat left word that she wouldn't be coming in to work then left a message on Alice's voice mail.

"She's going to call you back?" Simon paced in the living room. "You can't just wait around for her to call."

"It's on a cell— *mobile* phone. I carry it with me." Nat held her smartphone on her open palm for him to see.

"Oh... I get it." He stared at her, at her cell phone in her hand. "That's a *phone?*"

"Get down to Tout Sweets." Georgie, pointed to the front door, ordering Nat. "You're going to Daine's anyway. You need those éclairs!"

Nat grabbed her purse, snagged the car fob and headed out. The drive to Tout Sweets wasn't bad at all. At least she enjoyed some peace and quiet since the ghosts didn't ride in the car with her. She even listened to some music. If Simon and Georgie had traveled with her, Nat thought they'd fight about who'd get to choose the music station.

11

NAT HAD NEVER been to Tout Sweets and it turned out that, although Georgie had raved about the bakery, she'd never been there, either. She had only sampled their wares.

Nat picked up the luscious aroma half-a-block away. She didn't need the large painted white sign with purple and gold lettering over the front door to tell her that this was the bakery.

Once inside, Georgie and Simon acted like the kids in the proverbial candy store, pressing their noses against the display cases. Thank goodness no one could see them or hear their begging for sugary delicacies they couldn't have. It would have been embarrassing.

Without having to deny them, Nat walked out of the shop with her éclairs in a lavender box, tied with a beautiful white ribbon, and tacked down with a gold-foil Tout Sweets sticker printed in a fancy scroll font.

After sliding the éclairs into the refrigerator, Nat checked her phone messages. Alice had returned her call, told her not to take any precious baking time by calling back. She said, yes, she and Greg, would love to have some éclairs and thank you for thinking of them and that she would be home after three.

There was a good hour before Nat had to leave for Alice's. It was a good thing she had some time because she needed to make alterations to the store bought pastries. Number one, the box would have to go. A normal pink pastry box was what she needed, two of them, and she had some, someplace. And two, she'd have to un-Tout Sweets each éclair.

"So what do we do now, wait?" Simon began nibbling at his fingernails and found the path in the living room he liked to walk. "I don't know if I can stand the suspense of not knowing if the scarves are there or not."

"You're not going to pace the whole time until we leave, are you?" Georgie scolded him.

"No one says you have to stay. I have to find some new boxes." Nat thought one of the bottom cabinets that they used as a storage area would be a good place to start.

"What's wrong with their box? I think it's pretty," Georgie said in that prissy way Nat had come to hate.

"It's pretty but they're specially made for their bakery. I can't show up with that as is and claim I made those éclairs." Nat pulled the lower cabinet doors open and knelt on the floor to search inside.

"Oh, I see." The thought must have never occurred to Georgie.

Within a few minutes, Nat found the generic pink boxes, folded them, and set them aside on the kitchen table. She pulled the lavender box from the fridge and glanced at the Tout Sweets gold embossed sticker and felt a pang of guilt before she opened the lid. Passing off their pastries as her own was nothing less than culinary fraud.

"I love those little white fleur-de-lis." Georgie stood beside Nat, admiring the neat line of pastries in the box.

"You and all the other Tout Sweets patrons." Nat understood the admiration for the bakery's identifiable gold-dusted, white chocolate molded moniker that sat on each pastry. Each was a tiny work of art. "It has to go."

"That's sad." The corners of Georgie's mouth turned down into a little pout.

"Sorry," Nat said without sympathy. She slid the box aside and separated the éclairs, the cream and the custard, onto different plates.

Simon stopped his pacing long enough to ask. "Do I have to be around for this?" He must have thought that this was the most boring waste of time.

"No," Nat said curtly.

"Then I'm going." He dissolved into thin air.

"Good," Georgie said with a nod of her head. "We don't need him here to bother us."

Us?

Nat glanced up at Georgie. If only she could get rid of the other person who didn't need to be here. "Stand back, will you?" She motioned Georgie aside, she wasn't about to walk through her to get to the counter. "I need some workspace."

After pulling out the tools she needed, Nat carefully removed the white chocolate fleur-de-lis and set them on a small plate where Georgie kept herself busy admiring their cuteness.

With a warmed knife, Nat smoothed the rough spot in the chocolate and finished off by piping a zigzag of white icing over the top, making them resemble a generic éclair before repacking them into two smaller, normal, pink boxes for delivery.

By the time Nat had finished her great confection caper, it was after two-thirty. She had to get on the road and make her deliveries.

NAT SHOWED UP at Alice's around three-thirty with a small

pink box in hand, containing two cream and two custard filled éclairs.

"Come in, come in." Alice welcomed Nat with a friendly smile and motioned her into the house. It wasn't a house, really. Alice and Greg lived in a tall, multi-residence building and their living space looked like it stretched over the entire floor.

Clean lines and free of clutter, Alice's home looked light, decorated in beige and apricot; bright, with its large windows, one just behind the baby grand piano with a high gloss finish that reflected light and simple, expensive furniture with simple, clean lines. Well, Greg was a doctor, after all. They probably could afford it.

"Holy-endless-hallway," Simon commented, his eyes went wide. "This place goes on forever."

"The scarves, Simon. Remember?" Georgette touched his arm to gain his attention. "Let's go. Natalie, you do your best—stall."

Stall?

"Do you mind?" Alice held her hands out, ready to take the éclairs. "I just want to take a peek."

"Sure." Nat handed the pink box over, still trying to figure out how she was going to stretch her visit.

Alice opened the box and smiled wide. "They're beautiful and they look delicious."

"Thank you," Nat replied. She couldn't keep from feeling guilty about taking credit for a bake she didn't make. It was all for a greater good. She hoped it was for a greater good, anyway. She was supposed to be *stalling*. "Would you mind tasting one? Just a little bite. I'm curious to know how you think they turned out."

By the expression on Alice's face Nat could tell that she wanted to, but shouldn't.

"It's the middle of the afternoon but–" Alice hesitated then smiled "—just a taste. A tiny taste wouldn't hurt." She led the way to the kitchen, and Nat was glad to see that it brought her farther into the home.

Alice opened the box and eyed the contents appreciatively. "Which one?"

"Your choice."

"Custard." Alice decided, pulling out a knife to slice off a piece for herself.

"That one, then." Nat pointed.

Alice cut a half inch off one end and poised the knife to slice a second piece. "You want some?"

Nat refused as kindly as she could.

"I know, you've been around them all day and it makes you sick just to look at them." Alice must have picked up on the whole smelling-cooking thing from her brother-in-law.

"Exactly. Why don't you just go ahead and tell me what you think."

Alice shot Nat a self-conscious glance, admitting that she was about to do something naughty before she slipped the small piece into her mouth.

Alice held her hand over her mouth as she chewed, then rolled her eyes. "Oh, my gosh." She licked her lips, making sure she hadn't missed any of the crumbs.

"Does it taste all right?"

"This is wonderful." Alice swallowed and eyed the remainder of the éclair she'd left in the box. "It's as good as Tout Sweets'."

"Really?" Nat smiled, it was a nervous smile, then swallowed hard. "What a compliment— that's really nice of you to say."

"Natalie," Simon came into the kitchen. "We can't get to the very back rooms. You've got to go farther into the house." He pointed toward the back with both hands, then strolled out the way he came.

"Well, I guess I need to get going. Do you mind if I make a pit stop before I head over to Daine's?"

"That lucky guy is getting a special delivery too." Alice licked the smudge of dark chocolate from her thumb and led Nat out of the kitchen, through the living room, and pointed down the hall-way. "It's the second door on the left."

"I drink so much water when I'm baking, must be the heat from the oven," Nat mumbled while heading down the hall. Sure, like that was a believable explanation. Why didn't she just keep her mouth shut?

Simon was already in the bathroom waiting for her. It was a powder room, actually, again in apricot and beige, matching the living room, with green accents.

"We've got all six scarves," Simon announced. "In one of the back rooms."

"I can go now, right?" Nat wanted to make sure Georgie had finished before she left because she wasn't planning a return trip. How could Nat talk herself back for a second visit? With a straw-berry shortcake? A peach cobbler?

"Georgie's seen all she needs to see. She's finished. Let's get out of here." Simon dissolved into thin air.

Nat waited a few minutes then flushed the toilet.

DAINE LIVED IN what Nat thought looked more like an old industrial than a residential area. She stepped out of the car and stared up at the apartment building.

"I can't believe it," Simon ranted, appearing next to her. "I thought there was a pretty good chance Dr. Greg would have been the one."

"Maybe that's what he wants you to think." Georgie matched Nat and Simon stride for stride up the stairs to the second floor.

"That he'd be the obvious choice but he isn't because in reality the down and dirty Daine might be the Cut-Throat Chef." Simon shrugged and looked from Georgie to Nat for support for the off-the-top-of-his-head theory.

Nat pushed the buzzer to the front door.

Daine answered, pulling the door open wide. "Cmm-enn," he mumbled around a mouthful of food then finally swallowed. "Sorry." He stepped back and waved her into the room.

Nat caught the scent of something mouthwatering. Spicy. Sweet. Barbeque-y. Delicious.

"Last minute taste testing," he explained and led the way to the kitchen. "Do you have time?"

"Sure." Nat took in the stark, tall-ceiling residence.

"Oh, my God, he lives in a warehouse." Georgie couldn't have sounded more appalled.

"What do you call this decor? Early American Stainless?" Simon's disdain came through crystal clear. "This is the most bizarre set up I've ever seen. How can he even call himself a real man? Where's the television?"

Nat liked it—this was a dream kitchen: a six-burner Wolf range, a Viking French door double wall ovens, with a 60" wide Viking side-by-side refrigerator. Some of the stainless cabinet doors had glass fronts. Daine's apartment was a commercial kitchen shrunk to a residential size, which pretty much dominated the place, with enough furniture around it making it someplace comfortable to live.

"Take a taste, what do you think?" Daine motioned to two plates on the stainless steel countertop.

"Oh, great." Simon rolled his eyes. "He gives you a choice: arsenic or cyanide."

It wasn't that Nat thought Daine had really poisoned the food but she did hesitate.

"I don't see the scarves anywhere." Nat heard Georgie say from the far side of the room.

"I marinated both of them for four hours but this one" — Daine pointed to the plate on Nat's right— "I thought I'd spray on a second glaze while it was on the grill. I think it gives it an extra kick."

"The only place with doors is the kitchen cabinet and this bathroom." Simon made sure Nat saw him pointing at the bathroom door with an exaggerated motion and a wink. "Just in case we need to talk."

"Nat?" Daine caught her attention. "Are you going to sample these?"

She glanced at him then the plates of food. "Oh, right." Then she swallowed. He handed her a fork. Nat rolled the utensil between her fingers and took her time choosing which piece of meat to spear.

"This side first, I think." Daine indicated the plate on her left. "It's the plain ole marinated and grilled."

Nat brought the chicken to her lips. "Hmm... smells good." She smiled.

"I'm going to check up there in that loft." Georgie stood at the foot of the narrow staircase. "I think it's the bedroom. Maybe he's hiding them."

Instead of climbing, Georgie rose straight up into the air. Nat watched her then caught Daine still staring at her out of the corner of her eye. She popped the chicken into her mouth.

"This is good." Nat swallowed. "Really good." It tasted more like teriyaki than barbeque, but it was definitely a type of barbeque sauce.

"Now try this one." He took the fork from Nat and fed her a piece of the chicken from the second plate.

The flavor hit Nat's palate with a sha-BAM before she could say delicious.

"What *is* this?" The second barbecue chicken was definitely better. Wow. "Is this the same marinade? No, it can't be. What did you do to this?"

"It's the same marinade but I sprayed it with one of my

sauces." He pointed to a bottle sitting on the counter. "It's something I threw together."

"Are you going to keep the recipe to yourself?" She glanced up at him. "It's not going to be a secret once you give out the ingredients on the air. And you know you have to."

Daine's face dropped. It seemed that he hadn't thought about that.

"I know how you are about divulging your secret sauces." Nat could just imagine the conflict he faced—the inventive chef versus keeping the viewing public happy. "If you're going to reveal it, maybe you should give it a name? Call it Daine's Grilling Sauce."

It took nearly a minute before he warmed to the idea. Publicity, even local fame had its cost. "Yeah. Maybe I should." He must have decided that making one of his precious recipes public was a small price to pay for a little local celebrity.

"What else is on the menu?" Nat popped another piece in her mouth and focused on Daine.

He straightened and pulled out a legal-sized paper tablet. A myriad of lists, words written in all sorts of directions with arrows, crossed outs, underlined and circled dishes in every corner of the page. Nat didn't know how he could even make out anything legible out of the mess.

"The segment is called, *Six Dishes in Sixty Minutes*." He told her and read: "Roasted red bell peppers, veggie and chicken kabobs, cheesy garlic bread, broccoli delight, summer-fresh cucumber salad, and brownie a la mode."

"It's going to take more than one hour to—"

The phone rang and he picked up his cell to answer. "Hello? Hey, Angelo, what's going on?" He paused. "That's great. By the way, just want you to know that Natalie Powell will be assisting me tomorrow morning."

Daine sent a glance Nat's way but she had no idea what it meant.

"Ok, sounds good. That's for the update. Thanks again, I appreciate the support." He hung up the phone.

"That was Angelo Dimico."

The head chef at Sam's.

"We got the okay to use the kitchen tomorrow. He says it's good publicity for the restaurant."

I'll be in Side Street Sam's kitchen? Cooking in Sam's kitchen? Me. Nat had to take a deep breath. It was a dream come true.

"I was trying to put in a good word for you but I don't think you need it."

"What?" That shook Nat out of her daydream. "What do you mean? What's going on?"

"I can't say." Daine tapped his lips with his finger as if a big secret might slip out. "I don't want to ruin the surprise."

Nat didn't like surprises. They were usually bad.

"It's not him. All the scarves are there." Georgie reported after appearing in the kitchen next to her brother. "He stuck the box I sent him in a corner, way far back in a corner. He didn't even open it to see what was inside."

He didn't do it. That's what Georgie was really saying.

Nat felt relieved and a whole lot safer in Daine's company. She didn't really think he was a killer.

"What are we going to do now?" Simon made himself at home on the sofa, a good-ly distance from the kitchen. Nat wished Georgie would join him.

"Well if it's not Daine or Greg, who else could it be? Who'd want to—" Georgie stopped.

"I guess we'll have to wait for the police to come up with something." Simon sighed and sank back into the cushions. "I can't believe we have to rely on the police."

Daine walked to the fridge and returned with two bowls. "Here, try these." He set them on the counter. One had a broccoli mixture and the other looked to be marinated cucumbers.

Nat tried the broccoli salad first.

"So tell me," Daine began, sounding as if he were doing a little detective work of his own. "Is there something wrong with the Bistro?"

Nat swallowed and against her will couldn't help but feel guilty. "What do you mean?"

"You're interviewing at Sam's and you were talking to my sister about hiring on as her personal chef." Daine popped a small broccoli floret in this mouth, acting as calm as if he were making dinner conversation. "Gotta be a reason why you're hunting for a new job."

"I'll tell you if you tell me why you have a different name than your brother. *Owens?*" It would take more than the presence of six cashmere scarves to convince Nat that he didn't have some sort of secret. "Shouldn't your name be Price?"

"All right." Daine swallowed and with a curt nod agreed. "My real last name is Price. But I don't feel right about using it. Never have." It was clear that being ignored by his father while growing up had affected him, made him bitter. "I don't want to be associated with him in any way. So I use my mother's maiden name. Owens."

"What about the inheritance?" Nat dipped into the cucumbers but kept a keen eye for his reaction.

"Well, you're asking a lot of questions," he said with a tilt of his head. "Doesn't matter. No, thanks. I don't want a penny." He motioned back and forth with his fork. "I'll donate it all to charity anyway."

"Georgie thought your father was unfair, too, tried to give you more, I hear."

"Ten thousand—a hundred thousand isn't going to make any difference to me. I was thinking Humane Society, Cancer Research, The Rainy Day Foundation."

"But now with Georgie... gone—" Nat hesitated to say dead

with Georgie only twenty feet away. "Won't you be getting a lot more money?"

Daine gave Nat a dark look. He wasn't happy about her bringing up the Price inheritance. "Yeah, but how much is half an empire?"

"Exactly." Nat knew she risked angering him. She'd seen his temper, experienced it firsthand. When in the kitchen he swore, yelled, threatened, and became very intimidating, but he never got violent. But here she wasn't sure what kind of behavior to expect from him. "Are we talking millions or billions?"

"It won't matter. I'll give it away and I'm sure that there will be a long line of takers." He made the words sound final, shutting the door on the subject of his family.

"I was never seriously looking for another job." Nat jumped to her part of the bargain which was: What was wrong with the Bistro? "I just talked to Georgie about food. We were never serious about me working for her. As for Sam's, the opportunity came up and... Who wouldn't want to work there?"

Something about her tone or her words made Daine's face soften. He didn't look angry anymore. Whoever said that music soothes the savage beast had better reconsider and take a look at bribing the beast with food.

"Fair enough." He seemed pleased enough with what she had to say. He set his fork down and rubbed his hands together. "How about if we pull out those éclairs you brought?"

He didn't wait for her to answer. Pulling the small pink box out of the fridge, Daine set it on the counter and opened the lid as if it were a long lost treasure from King Tut's tomb. You'd have thought he'd never seen an éclair before.

"Cream or custard?" he asked, opening a drawer and pulled out a dinner knife.

"Your choice." Heaven forbid Nat should say the wrong thing.

"Cus-stard," he said. The S came out in a long, exaggerated

hiss. Delving into the box, his eyes and hands moved with the precision of a neurosurgeon and sliced a piece the éclair for her and a second piece for himself.

Nat popped her morsel into her mouth while Daine moved with reverence, taking his time before wrapping his taste buds around the sample. His eyes slid shut and experienced the flavor and wonderful texture of the pastry.

"Do you think they're as good as Tout Sweets?" Nat made a preemptive strike. If anyone was going to mention the bakery it was going to be *her* this time.

"No." Daine finished chewing and smiled. "They're better. Much, much better."

NAT WAS SO excited about filming the TV show that she'd awaken hours before Daine arrived to pick her up. She was even awake before Georgie and Simon could show up to bug her.

Excited was putting it mildly. Thrilled, ecstatic, those weren't the right words either. Nat felt beyond happy and beyond... she was over the moon.

"You'll never guess what happened when I got home last night." Nat bounced down the front stairs of her apartment building behind Daine when he showed up at five in the morning.

"You had a message on your answering machine?" He wasn't guessing, he already knew, and he was taking all the fun out of her news. "From Angelo."

"Was that the 'surprise' you were talking about last night?" Nat stopped at the curb next to his car.

"Nice, was it?" Bleep. The car unlocked with the press of a button. "I'm excited for you. You're one of three applicants left and I think you have a good shot at getting the job. I'm rooting for you."

"I'm secretly hoping that helping you out today will give me an edge," Nat confessed after she slid into the passenger's seat.

"It couldn't hurt." Daine started the car and pulled into the light traffic.

"You wouldn't by any chance have a say in—" Nat hated to think she'd gotten the job with a slightly unfair advantage, namely Daine, but...

"I've already had my input at the first interview. It's up to Dimico now. I was just letting him know that I have enough confidence in you to assist me today." Daine glanced at Nat out of the corner of his eye and gave her a small smile. "As I said, it couldn't hurt."

He was on her side. A mixed sense of pride and guilt passed over her. How could she have ever thought that he could have murdered Georgie? He wasn't exactly heartless but he didn't really know his half-sister.

And he wasn't interested in her money. What he really cared about was food and cooking. He'd told her so last night. And maybe, just maybe he cared about having Nat working in the same kitchen, alongside him, too. Wouldn't that be nice?

"Have you heard from the police yet?" she asked.

"What?"

All right, it was a question out of the blue. He was probably thinking about today, about being on television, and what had to be done. He'd been working, eating, and sleeping his menu. If he got any sleep, that is. The police and Georgie's murder were probably the last thing on his mind.

"I was just wondering if there's been any word about Georgie's case or if they'd gotten any test results back." Nat felt the atmosphere inside the car change, grow colder, despite the sun coming up.

"No. I haven't heard a thing." Daine's voice sounded gruff

from his displeasure at the change of topic. Or maybe the return to an unpleasant topic. Why had she gone there?

Nat couldn't make herself meet his gaze. She stared at her hands, resting on her lap and studied her fingernails with great interest. "I guess no news is good news."

There was no response.

"Well," she continued and cleared her throat. "Do you want to tell me what we're doing today?"

He gave her a curt nod and began, "I'll give you a rundown. When we get to Sam's...."

Daine had planned to make three sets of each dish: one in its raw state, the second at the cooking stage, and the third in a finished, ready-to-eat product.

Nat paid close attention. Daine listed, in order, what he wanted her to do. Once they stepped into the kitchen they could get straight to work.

Arriving at Sam's, Daine parked the car and Nat followed him in the back entrance. He'd been quiet during the ride. She hoped she hadn't angered him. That's all she needed, the emergence of what Simon had called The Cut-Throat Chef.

Daine pointed for Nat to go to the right when they stepped through the door. She stopped in her tracks. She was in the kitchen. Sam's kitchen.

Gleaming stainless steel as far as the eye could see, the counters, the now-bare serving shelves that would be teeming with plates piled high with plenty of palate-pleasing perfection twelve hours from now.

But something was out of place. Something was wrong. In front of her, sitting on the stainless counter before her was a brown hat. A familiar looking hat, one she hadn't seen in a long time. Brown with a narrow brim.

Mitch's? Was he back? Here?

Nat's gaze swept the kitchen, searching for any other signs of him. She heard the faint rattling of metal. Pots, pans or was it something else?

Again Nat thought of Mitch and the special talent he had with metallic objects.

"Get your crap out of here!" Daine's voice boomed from behind Nat, scaring her half to death. "Juan!"

Juan came running out of nowhere. "Sorry, boss." He swept his hat off the counter and ran out of the kitchen. Seconds later, he'd returned, tying on an apron.

The hat wasn't Mitch's, it was Juan's.

"Come on, let's get started." Daine handed Nat an apron and brushed by her.

Okay. So Nat's first experience in Sam's kitchen wasn't a great one. She'd angered Daine which would make him prickly company for both her and Juan. This was just bad and Nat hoped it wouldn't get any worse.

"Sorry, we're late." Simon appeared next to her.

"Eww, a kitchen." Georgie cowered next to Simon as if he could save her from the drudgery. The expression on her face looked as if she were standing in the dumpster.

"What do we do first?" Simon all but rolled up his shirtsleeves ready to plunge into the tasks ahead.

"Could use some help here, Nat," Daine called out. He was turning into his alter-ego... the Cut-Throat Chef. "Let's go. COME ON!"

A FEW HOURS in the kitchen mellowed Daine. It seemed to Nat that his anger had evaporated, replaced by stage fright. He'd lost the growl in his voice and soon he was saying nothing at all. It felt odd and sort of scary. The one good thing about the approaching airtime was that he seemed to forget all about her asking him about Georgie's murder and the police investigation.

And she wasn't about to bring it up anytime soon. She'd learned that lesson.

Nat and Daine had both changed into a black-piped, V-necked gray chef's coat that the restaurant's kitchen staff wore. She donned the red-logoed Sam's black baseball cap, slipping her short ponytail through the back, and picked up the coordinated kerchief and slipped it around her neck.

"Hey, let me help." Daine took the ends of the kerchief and placed one side over the other, wrapping the one end around, pulling it through, partially tying the knot. "We're going to do great."

Nat noticed that he'd said *we,* not *he.*

"Daine..." Feeling a constricting at her throat, she coughed. "Ah... Daine...."

"Oh, no," Simon warned, pointing, wide-eyed, at Daine's work. "Georgie, do something."

"I can't do anything." She did stand next to Simon and shout out more warnings. "Watch it. He's ch-choking—choking you."

Nat grabbed at her neck. She knew. She could feel it. But why... why?

"I'm sorry," Daine whispered, growing more uncomfortable and agitated as the seconds ticked by. He continued to fiddle with it.

What was he doing? Nat couldn't breathe. Was this because she'd brought up Georgie's murder? Was this because he thought that Nat thought he was a killer?

"There's a problem here." Daine pushed her hands away from her neck and held them down.

"He's got a knife!" Simon shouted. Nat glanced around and couldn't see a thing.

"Oh, God—a knife!" Georgie repeated.

"Hold still," Daine said in complete calm and a bit forcefully.

He had a knife. Nat still couldn't see him. Simon's panicked tone caught her by surprise and she would have screamed bloody murder if she could get a lungful of air.

Was this payback? But she hadn't thought he did it. Nat had been sure, or pretty sure, anyway. Until now. She kept twisting... trying to see....

Then she caught the harsh bright fluorescent light glinting from the nine-inch blade, blinding her as he brought it near her face and moved it toward her ear. Nat struggled against him again, still feeling the stranglehold he had around her neck.

"Wha... whaaaat..." she tried to say, but no words came out. She promised never, ever to talk to him about Georgie's death again. Nat wouldn't, ever. Never.

Please stop.

"Hold still," he repeated.

The cool blade slid against her neck. Nat felt the slight pressure of metal dig into her skin. She felt a momentarily tightening around her neck before the hiss of splitting cloth, then release from the kerchief from around her neck.

Nat took a deep breath. Tears moistened her eyes with her second breath of air.

"Sorry," Daine said, replacing the knife into the block. "It knotted up, I couldn't loosen the knot."

Nat nodded. "It's okay," she whispered and rubbed her throat. A little scary, though. But everything was all right, and he hadn't tried to kill her.

Simon collapsed into an invisible chair and rubbed his face. He looked almost as frightened as she felt. "I thought he was going to slit you from ear to ear."

Simon wasn't the only one thinking that. The same thought had crossed Nat's mind.

"Here's another one." Daine handed Nat a second kerchief.

"Don't worry about this one" —he dropped the first one in the trash— "there are plenty."

Nat wrapped the kerchief around her neck, albeit very loosely, and tied it before Daine could even make an offer to help. That kind of help she did not need.

"Daine?" Someone wearing a headset and holding a clipboard traipsed into the kitchen. "We'll be ready for you in ten."

12

A WARM, SUNNY afternoon made a perfect backdrop for the outdoor kitchen that sat in the middle of Union Square across the street from Side Street Sam's.

Daine stood behind the counter and Steve Strider, one of Evening Magazine's co-hosts introduced himself and shook his hand. A third man approached the two.

"Ah, the director," Simon announced.

"What do you know?" Georgie's snotty attitude made it clear that she did not want to be here. Nat wondered why she hadn't just left.

"This is all exactly the way I remember it." Simon sighed, looking as if he were reminiscing about the good ole days of his own television show.

The director pointed and gestured with his arms, instructing the men on where to stand and which camera to look into. Nat rechecked the food placement for each dish and checked off the last minute mental details.

"Wait a sec," he said. Daine flagged Nat and she turned toward him. "Dave, this is Natalie Powell. She'll be assisting me today."

"Natalie." Dave greeted her with a smile and a curt nod. "Steve Strider."

"Nice to meet you," Nat replied, taking a moment to acknowledge him then returning to her work.

"How about the brownies?" Simon called out to Nat, peering into the small window on the oven. "You haven't forgotten them, have you?"

Nat pulled the door open to let Simon see for himself that she hadn't forgotten the precooked dessert as she walked by on her way to the other side of the set.

"Take your places," someone called out. "Now quiet, everyone." Another person ran in front of the camera, quickly rambled off something before snapping a clapboard and dashing out of the way.

"Remember this is *live*, people!" the director said. "And action!"

Steve introduced Daine as the local hot-celebrity chef and gave Side Street Sam's a nice bit of promotion. Some of the crew clapped, encouraging the ten or so onlookers into a round of polite applause.

"Six dishes in sixty minutes—are you sure? Is that really possible?" Steve made a half-hearted argument at the impossibility of the task.

"The cooking part can be done, my friend, but the secret is in the preparations. They're done a day ahead, which gives you plenty of time without added pressure. The day of your party can be spent with your guests instead of being trapped in your kitchen."

"Okay, you're the man with the apron." Steve stepped back, giving Daine room to work. "Show us."

Daine explained the menu and what could be done before the party. Starting with dessert, he heated the ice cream mixture on the stovetop and left it to cool to room temperature before storing it in the refrigerator.

Next, he trimmed the broccoli florets, cut the veggies and meat for kabobs, and mixed the spring cucumber salad, instructing that it should sit in the fridge overnight to marry the flavors.

"Look at that." Simon stood glued in front of the monitor. "The camera loves him."

Georgie glanced at the screen before shrugging. "Who cares? This is a teeny, nothing, local show."

"Well, Miss Know-It-All, for your information, teeny, nothing local shows can lead to big, important shows that are aired nation-wide. That's how I started out." Simon relayed as a guy who's already been through it.

Daine's instructions for the morning of the party were to mari-nate the kabob meat and veggies between two and four hours. Mix the brownies and bake. Place the ice cream mixture in the maker and when that finished, place it into the freezer to set. Assemble the kabobs by alternating the meat and vegetables on the skewers.

"Now it's time" —Daine said pointedly to Steve— "to turn on the fire."

"My favorite part." Steve rubbed his hands together, showing his excitement. "Where's my apron?"

Nat slid the spare apron across the counter toward Steve. He whispered an on-camera thanks and tied it around his waist.

Daine had started the gas grill and talked about roasting the red bell peppers, blackening the skin on all sides. He handed Steve a pair of tongs and put him in charge while he laid the kabobs on the grill.

When Steve had finished with the peppers, they were placed in a bowl and covered with cellophane to steam in their own heat for about twenty minutes. Daine spritzed the kabobs with a glaze then turned them. Fire licked the skewers and made a crackling sound, sending fresh waves of delicious barbecue scent into the air.

"Don't spray this into the fire," Daine warned then sent a blast of spray into the flames, orange flares shot from the grill a foot high.

"Okay." Steve leaned away from the fire. "The glaze stays on the food. What's in that bottle, by the way?"

"You'll find the recipe for the glaze" —Daine held up the spray bottle— "along with the rest of the dishes on your website."

"They'll be putting that on the screen right below us." Steve pointed downward where the words would appear.

The grilling aroma drifted through the air, enticing more and more people to join the audience. Nat guessed there must have been close to fifty onlookers.

"What are they looking at?" Georgie didn't sound as if she appreciated the crowd that was gathering around the roped-off cooking area.

"Will you look at that?" Simon shifted his attention from the monitor to the crowd, now three deep and growing. "They're drawn to him like bees to honey."

"Or like flies to garbage." Georgie's cynical tone hadn't changed.

Simon shot Georgie a sharp look. "He's your brother. You should want him to be a success."

In a matter of minutes, Daine had presented plate after plate after plate of the finished items: the roasted red peppers, the veggie/chicken kabobs, the cheesy garlic bread, the cucumber salad, the broccoli delight, and finally the homemade vanilla ice cream plated next to a piece of chewy brownie.

"All right. It can be done." Steve held up his hands, giving in. "You did it. Amazing, but how does it taste?"

Steve, with a fork in hand, pulled the first plate toward him, taking his time tasting each dish and savoring every bite before doing a short commentary about each.

Daine finally announced that they had samples for the audience which was a big crowd-pleaser. Nat, with Juan's help, brought out the samples and began passing them around.

The director yelled, "Cut! Print it. That's a wrap." The action on the stage continued. People approached the counter, introducing themselves to Daine, talking to him, and asking for autographs.

Nat thought the cooking demonstration was a success. Good exposure for Daine, good experience for her, and a great opportunity for the restaurant that must have gotten a huge publicity boost when Daine scrawled his name on Sam's take-out menus and gave them away by the dozens.

DAINE WASN'T THE ogre she had remembered. Not counting the little knife mishap before the show, they'd worked in splendid harmony. *Sam's* kitchen staff, who was just coming on duty, took care of the majority of the clean-up from the show prep. Nat and Daine packed up some of the leftovers and placed it in the trunk of Daine's car.

Nat walked with Daine from *Sam's* kitchen to leave.

"Tired?" he asked.

"Yeah, but a good tired." Nat relaxed in the seat, having the satisfying feeling that she'd taken part in something worthwhile.

"You did a great job."

"So did you." Nat wanted to say more but she didn't want to gush or sound overly flattering. But he really had impressed her. He'd come across wonderfully on television.

"Are you in a hurry to get home?"

Nat felt that adrenaline euphoria that came after a night's work rush and couldn't imagine what else Daine might have in mind.

"I want to stop by my Mom's to drop off some of the extra

food." He glanced over at her. His hands were wrapped around the steering wheel and he stared at them as if felt a little nervous. "You wouldn't want to go with me, would you?"

That would mean driving past her house and spending hours in the car with him instead of hitting the shower and stretching out on the sofa at home to kick back for the night. Nat did not find the thought of spending time with Daine all that unpleasant.

"Sure," Nat said, hoping he'd relax his grip on the steering wheel and smile. "Is that what was loaded into your car?"

"She's planning on sharing with the neighbors," Daine explained and started the engine "—everyone who lives within a mile's radius."

NAT MOVED TO the back of the Mustang where Daine stood but wasn't there alone for long.

"What are we doing here?" Simon stood next to Nat, facing Marian Price's house. "Again."

"Oh, good. I'm glad we're back." Georgie sounded happier than she had all day. "There's something in there I wanted to take a second look at."

"What are you talking about?" Simon scolded her. "We've already been through this house."

"But there's one place I couldn't see last time. It was too dark."

"Nat?" Daine held out an armful of take-out for her to carry.

"Oh, sorry." Nat took the box from Daine. "I guess I'm kind of zoned."

"No problem." He hefted a second box, closed the trunk, and headed up the walk to the house.

Nat followed him inside and into the kitchen.

"Come on, let's take a look," Simon whispered to Georgie. Nat glanced over her shoulder at the two of them and watched them leave the kitchen.

"I'll leave Mom a note, tell her we stopped by bearing gifts." Daine set his box on the counter. "We can leave the brownies out but we'll stick everything else in the fridge."

"We should put the ice cream in the freezer." Nat set her box on the counter next to Daine's and sorted through the containers for the brownies and ice cream.

"If you can find it."

"It'll leave a mess if we don't." Nat found the ice cream. "Here it is." She stuck the containers in the freezer.

"Georgie needs you back there." Simon pleaded with Nat. "You've got help her."

Nat glanced back at Daine, wondering how she could step away without being noticed. Or maybe she should use her "bathroom" excuse again.

Daine's cell phone rang. "Hello?"

"It's your chance. Go now." Simon urged her. "I'll keep watch."

"But what if—" Nat whispered.

"I'll stay here." Simon waved her out.

Nat went down the hall, keeping an eye out for Georgie.

"In here." Georgie stepped into the hallway and waved Nat into Marian Price's bedroom.

Nat glanced back toward the kitchen. Her heart pounded, nearly out of her chest, she felt nervous, anxious as she watched for a warning from Simon that Daine was off the phone.

"It's in there. I need you to look inside. I have a feeling it's important." Georgie pointed at the old accordion-door closet. "I have a feeling it's something odd, but it's too dark to see what it is."

Nat took another look over her shoulder, down the hall,

making sure Daine was nowhere to be seen before she pulled the doors open.

"Oh, my G—" Nat gasped, her eyes shot wide open. The shock of the closet's contents knocked her backward.

"It's Daddy." Georgie's voice choked with emotion. Her eyes widened, she stared from one side of the closet to the other, taking it all in. "It's... They're all pictures of Daddy."

A shrine—that was the only word for it. It was an altar, a place to worship the man whose 8x10 picture sat in the middle of the smaller photos and mementos of a younger Marian and George Price, during happier days that must have been over thirty years ago.

She loved him. Maybe even still loved him.

Nat just stared. She had a hard time tearing her gaze away from the pictures, the trinkets that had come from across the globe—a tiny Eiffel Tower statue and the Leaning Tower of Pisa. The Great Wall of China ran from the left side to the right, running behind a miniature Edinburgh Castle. As strange as this global mishmash was, the thing that caught her eye hung just to the left side.

A clear garment bag, containing what looked like it might be a coat and one of George Price's infamous cashmere scarves. So Marian Price also had one. Maybe she had more than one.

"She's a sicko," Georgie said in disgust.

"She seemed so normal, so nice." Nat still had trouble imagining Marian Price responsible for this bizarre memorial-shrine thing.

"They must be in it together, her and Daine," Georgie said it with complete certainty. "Maybe it's all three of them. Greg's in with them, too."

A sudden gust of air blew against Nat's face, making her blink against it.

"You have to leave." Simon was there, standing next to her, gesticulating wildly. "Get out of here now. Right now!"

"Is he coming?" Georgie moved away from the shrine, panic had set in and it showed on her face.

"No, he's still on the phone. That Detective, Holland, he's saying that they have a match, a DNA match and the fingerprints in the passage are his, too. Daine's."

"What?" Nat couldn't believe it. Daine's DNA? And his fingerprints?

"It's him. He's the killer." Simon's words came tumbling out. "You have to get out of the house."

Nat ran down the hall and stopped just outside the kitchen. Daine was still talking on the phone. She peeked around the corner to see him.

Georgie's killer... Daine. Nat still couldn't believe it.

"I'm telling you it's impossible. I never even knew that passageway was there," he swore to Holland.

"He's arguing with the police, do you hear that?" Simon shouted. "You gotta get out now!"

Leave? Yeah, leaving was a good idea. How could she get away?

"Take his car," Simon told her, urging her to make her move. "His keys are in his right front pocket."

Take his car keys? How could she do that? There was no way Nat could get by him, much less *take* his keys from him.

"Use the frying pan." Simon pointed to the stovetop.

Frying pan? Nat mouthed.

"You know." Simon mimicked swinging it like a bat, hitting a home run.

No. She couldn't.

Her disbelief must have been written all over her face. She felt warm, hot, flushed. Nat's heart was beating so hard. What should she do?

"Go on, go ON!" Simon urged.

"Well, your lab boys must have made a mistake. My fingerprints couldn't be in that passage. I've never been in there, ever."

Daine was still arguing, denying Detective Holland's facts. "You'd better have them recheck their test results because they're wrong."

Simon was right, Nat had to get out of there. And if it meant stealing—*borrowing* Daine's car so be it.

Simon motioned for Nat to make her move.

Nat took a deep breath before she stepped into the kitchen. In one fluid movement, she grasped the handle of the pan and swung it around, over her head and brought it down on Daine's head with a resounding *THUNK*.

"Sorry." Nat squeaked and watched him stop speaking mid-sentence. He stood there silent and motionless for a fraction of a second before he and his phone crumpled to the ground.

"Front right pocket," Simon repeated, sounding nervous for her.

Nat replaced the skillet on the cooktop and knelt next to Daine to retrieve his car fob.

"Don't worry, the police will come and take him away." Simon urged her on and out of the house. "Go on, get out of here before he wakes up."

"He is going to be all right, isn't he?" Nat didn't want to think she'd killed him.

"He's going to be fine, don't worry." Simon waved her on. "Now, go. Go!"

Nat didn't take time to think, she just ran. Simon was right. She had to get out of there, and the sooner she heard sirens approaching, the better.

She jumped into Daine's Mustang and locked the doors. After snapping on the seat belt, she started the car and pulled away from the curb, heading for safety down the street.

Now what? Where was she going? It didn't matter. She just needed to get away. The farther away she was from Daine, the safer she would be.

SMASH! Someone hit her from behind, Nat was knocked

forward. It was some crazy person in a car behind her. They must be drunk or something.

SMASH! Metal to metal screeched when the bronze-colored car trailed dangerously close to her bumper. They were trying to crash into her again.

Nat tightened her hold on the steering wheel and swerved to miss a parked station wagon and swerved back to the right to get her out of the middle of the road.

The bronze car moved around Nat's and veered into her lane. There was a CRASH and SCREECH—sideswiping the Mustang with a horrible high pitched scraping noise.

That person was not fooling around, they were really trying to hurt her.

She was going to die. Nat couldn't help but put on the gas to try and get out of the way, but it wasn't working. She tapped the brake, hoping to keep control of the car.

The car swung into her lane again, this time making contact and pushed Nat straight into a tree, and that's when everything went black.

13

THE HOSPITAL DOOR swung open, surprising Simon. Had he been corporeal, and paying more attention, he would have jumped out of the way. As it was, he felt mesmerized by the blinking lights and the bleeps of the medical machinery and let Greg Price walk through him.

"What are you doing here? The hospital called and said you were hurt. I ran out straight over here from my office." Greg, still in his white doctor's coat, tried to catch his breath. "By the time I got to the ER, they said you were up here." He stared at Daine who stood at Natalie's bedside. "For God's sake—I thought you might be—"

"Nat could have been killed, Greg," Daine whispered. "That was no *accident* she was in."

"You'd better take it easy." Greg eyed the blood-soaked bandage around Daine's head but didn't seem inclined to touch it. Simon thought it was an odd reaction, didn't this doctor have any empathy for his own brother? "You'll need to have that taken care of."

"I will, later. I'm okay for now. I need to make sure Nat is all right."

Greg pulled his younger brother away from Natalie's bedside and forced him into a chair. "The least you can do is sit."

"I'm fine." Daine shrugged Greg's hand off his shoulder but never took his eyes from Natalie's bruised and swollen face. "I've cut my finger a lot worse with a paring knife."

He really cared for her. Simon could tell.

"Is her family here?" the brother wanted to know.

"They've already called her sister and she's on her way." Daine shot a threatening look at Greg. "But I'm not leaving her side."

"You don't have to leave." Greg sounded as if he were doing his best not to upset his brother. "You'd better have someone look at that goose egg." He probed at it and Daine winced. "I think it might need a couple of stitches."

"Good thing it's only your head, you might have been hurt," Simon and Greg chorused. Simon turned his head to look at Greg and wondered what the heck made that happen. There was an eerie silence during the few moments that followed. Not one of the medical machines even beeped.

"Do you think she knows I'm here?" Daine scooted his chair closer and laid his hand on Natalie's.

"I don't know." Greg didn't come anywhere near to the compassion of *Grey's Anatomy's* Dr. McDreamy.

Simon groaned. Didn't this guy have *any* bedside manners? He seemed as compassionate as a lump of clay and Daine was his own brother.

"*I* think she knows." Daine sounded way more positive than Greg. "We don't want to upset her. She has to rest and then she'll wake up."

"Daine...."

Simon could tell Greg wanted to say that it didn't work like that.

"I'll call Alice and let her know that you'll be staying with us for a couple of days."

"What for?" Daine didn't sound as if he were going anywhere. He was going to stay put. "I'm not leaving Nat."

"You shouldn't be alone." That was more like it. Not only did Greg speak as a doctor, he sounded like an older, caring brother.

"I'm at the hospital. If I pass out, they can stick me in the bed next to hers." No, he wasn't going to budge. Daine made that perfectly clear. Apparently clear enough for even Greg to get the message.

Greg cleared his throat. "By the way, the police are going to want to talk to you."

"Me? About what?" Daine hadn't been near the car accident. Was it because his car was involved?

"You're going to want to talk to them, too. Things have kind of taken a nasty turn." Greg wore the strangest expression and if Daine had been looking at his brother instead of Natalie he might have noticed. "You wouldn't believe—"

The door inched open. It was Becca. *Thank goodness!* Simon was so relieved to see her.

"Oh, my God, Nat!" She looked from Greg to Daine to Natalie in the bed, lying deathly still. "What happened to her? Is she all right? Why is she just lying there?"

Daine went to Becca to calm her. "Shh, don't wake her, she needs her rest. Let's step outside for a sec, okay?" He led her back out the door and Greg followed. "You don't want Nat seeing you like this."

Simon watched the three of them leave. He stayed and looked down at Natalie.

Poor, poor Natalie. This was his fault. Simon just knew that he had killed her.

Simon stood at the end of Natalie's bed and took in the sight of all the tubes and wires that strung from her to the buzzing and beeping machines, monitoring her vital signs.

She wasn't dead. Not yet, but she hung somewhere in between. And it could happen.

Please save her. Simon pleaded in silence. He pressed his hands together, as close to prayer hands as he'd ever made. *Someone, please save her life.*

The nauseating, pseudo-calming pale yellow walls of the ICU room blurred. The muted, pastel color bled away leaving it a soft gray. Simon squeezed his eyes closed. He was in a new place, an empty place. He saw nothing and sensed nothing around him.

He was to blame, this was all his fault. He couldn't stop thinking about it. The mounting guilt gnawed at him. Natalie should have never taken the car. She should have never been on the road. She never should have listened to him.

Simon was sorry. So, so sorry.

The guilt hurt inside. But that couldn't be. He couldn't feel physical pain. He shouldn't have, anyway. It wasn't possible. He must have been dreaming.

He would have taken her place in an instant—but... Oh, right... that wouldn't work, he was already dead.

If someone could only save her.

Simon had learned his lesson. He'd shut up, keep his big trap shut. Now he got it. Really got it—understood what he'd done wrong.

He'd shot off his mouth more times than he could remember. It was a reflex. He'd never thought about what he said first, he just said it, right off the top of his head.

He'd encouraged his sister to go to New York to seek her fortune on the Great White Way. It had been the brotherly thing to do. He hadn't kept in touch and didn't find out, until five years later, that she'd made it big in prostitution, not the Broadway stage. After several years of drugs and street life, she'd killed herself.

He'd cost Michelle her life. Simon knew that for certain now. Their Aunt Edith had thought so from the very beginning. *I told* him that Michelle should have gotten married and had kids and never left the safety of Cincinnati and the family who loved her.

Then there was Mike the cameraman who worked on Simon's television show. Simon had told Mike to do what would make him happy. What should have been a personal decision became the right for standing up for one's self in Simon's head without regard to those around him, namely Mike's family.

Simon should have kept out of Mike's life.

Mike had left his wife and kids for his twenty-two year old girl-friend. After Mike had gone, his family had to move out of their home. He'd left them and he'd left Simon's show, never to be seen again. Mike's wife lived on welfare and raised their three sons by herself. Only one made it to adulthood. But not far—he died at the age of twenty-one.

How many other people had he hurt? How many had he given his thoughtless advice? Any thought of the consequences, whom it hurt, or what had happened after he'd put in his two cents never occurred to him.

He clutched his chest and pressed, the new-found guilt felt like a knife piercing his heart. He wanted it to stop.

His knees weakened and he eased himself toward the floor. Next time, if there were ever a next time, he'd keep his mouth closed. He'd keep his half-baked ideas to himself. He would think before speaking.

What a foolish, brainless being he'd been. An unthinking idiot.

He could see now how dearly his thoughtlessness had cost Natalie and Simon had been responsible. She would have never hit Daine with the frying pan if he hadn't told her. She would have never taken the keys to his car. And she would have never been in that accident which caused her to now lie in this bed.

Indecision wasn't a crime and bullying people into taking action wasn't always the best thing to do. He knew that now. Why hadn't anyone ever told him to shut up?

Why didn't anyone tell him to mind his own business and keep his nose out of their affairs? Why had anyone ever listened to him? Because for whatever reason, people liked him and people listened to him and, more times than not, they had taken his advice.

Poor Natalie. He didn't want anything to happen to her. What he needed to do now was help Georgie find who killed her. That's all that was left for him to do; that was all that mattered.

He'd hurt so many people with his unwanted advice. Was there no way to correct his errors? Could he fix what he'd done wrong?

Too late. The words came to him loud and clear.

It was too late.

Simon would never, ever forgive himself.

It wasn't fair that Natalie had to pay the price because of him. If he had to do it over again... if he had his life to relive....

Simon closed his eyes and pressed his hands to his face. Would it, could it ever be fixed? Was it possible?

What Simon needed was a second chance.

NAT OPENED HER eyes.

She laid flat on her back with bright white light shining all around her and she couldn't tell where it was coming from. Strange. It was neither warm nor cold.

Where was she? What had happened? The last thing she remembered was... was...

Nothing. She couldn't remember. How long had she been here?

She tried to move. Was she lying on a table? On the floor? She rolled to her side and then dropped her legs toward the floor and sat up, but it didn't seem as if she were sitting on anything at all. The best she could guess was that she had been floating in mid-air.

Looking around her, she couldn't see any discernible walls or ceiling.

What kind of place was this?

Once on her feet, she took a step, then two, and then a dozen before stopping. It didn't seem that she'd moved any farther from where she'd started.

Not only could she not see where she was going, she couldn't tell in which direction she'd come. Everything, bathed in pristine white, looked the same. She had no idea how long she'd been wandering. A few minutes? Or maybe closer to an hour.

"Natalie?" a familiar man's voice called to her. "Natalie, is that you?"

She looked around with no real sense of direction, much less of any difference between near or far. Then *he* appeared.

Mitch.

He looked exactly the same as the last time she'd seen him. Wearing the same suit and carrying the same hat he hated so much, he tossed it aside before he reached her.

"Natalie." His large, warm hand surrounded hers and he pulled her close to embrace her.

He felt wonderful, familiar, comforting but... he *touched* her.

If a dead person could touch her did that mean.... she was...

Her eyes shot wide open, she leaned away and tried to pull her hand from his. "Mitch?"

She glanced at their clasped hands. What the heck did this mean? Something had happened, something had changed. And Nat had the feeling it was not for the better.

"Am I— Am I...." She couldn't say it.

"Dead? No." But the serious timber of his voice let her know that this was no joke. "You shouldn't be here."

"Here? Where is here?" Nat had been trying to figure that out for what seemed like forever. If Mitch could provide an answer she'd be ever-so-grateful.

"I can't tell you." He didn't sound as if he didn't want to tell her but as if he didn't know.

"But you're here." And had he been here the entire time? In a place that he didn't know where? Trapped here? "Where have you been? We needed you."

"I'm sorry. I don't have any answers for you." He shrugged.

"What about Georgie and Simon?" Nat glared at him in anger more than fear. The expression on his face was blank as if he had no idea who or what she was talking about. "But you remember me, right? What about Daine?"

"Daine...." The momentary recognition flickered across his face before he shook it off. "There is nothing I can do." His voice grew stern. "All I know is that you shouldn't be here."

Nat saw a sparkling light, shining just off to one side of them, where Mitch had come. "What's that?" She felt a pull toward it. She wanted to go there, see what it was.

Mitch looked over his shoulder to see what Nat was staring at. "No, it's not your time. You have to go back."

"Back? Back where?" Nat had no idea how to do that. And there was a beautiful light, beckoning her.

"You don't want to go that way," Mitch warned. "Please," the plea came out harsh. His hold on her relaxed and he stepped away from her. "Turn around and walk back the same way you came."

Nat turned reluctantly from him and faced in the opposite direction. She turned back, toward him. "What about you? You look...." *Ill* is what she wanted to say but how could a dead person look sick?

He urged her forward with a curt nod.

Nat finally turned away, free from his grasp, and took one step and then another. She paused again to glance at him over her shoulder.

"I don't know what's going to happen" —Fear tinged his fading voice— "to either of us."

14

"DID YOU SEE that? I think she opened her eyes," a man said. "Nat? Natalie? Can you hear me?"

Nat heard the man's voice but it wasn't Mitch's.

"I think she's trying to open her eyes," a woman said. "There, look— she did it again."

That voice sounded familiar too.

"Did you see that?" the man said. "Nat? Natalie? Can you hear me?"

"Push the button. Call the nurse." The woman insisted, her pitch rising in a pleased but agitated way.

"I've already pushed it. Where are they?" The man sounded impatient. "You stay with her. I'm going to find someone."

Nat heard quick, heavy footsteps move away and the door swing open, then closed as he left. She kept struggling to open her eyes, but her lids were nearly impossible to move. Finally, she managed to crack them open.

"Thank goodness, you're back." Becca stared down at her. It was Becca, Nat recognized her right away. "I'm so happy you're awake."

Nat may have been awake but she felt so out of it, disconnected. Where was she? What had happened? She couldn't remember much and her brain felt fuzzy.

Opening her mouth proved impossible. She lay on her back as she had before when she woke the first time, in the white place.

The white place... she barely remembered anything about it now. It seemed so long ago.

Here light-colored yellow walls surrounded her, unlike the last room. The last room...why had she thought of that? Had it been important?

The door opened and three people rushed in, surrounding her. Hospital personnel. They pushed Becca to the side, away from the bed.

"You'll have to wait in the hallway, Miss," a dark-haired man dressed in blue scrubs said to Becca.

A blonde, pony-tailed woman with tropical foliage and red parrot print top bustled around to the opposite side and pressed the buttons on a machine.

"I'll be right outside, okay?" Becca said to Nat. "When they're finished I'll come back. I promise."

"Miss, please, step outside, now," the second insisted, almost escorting her to the door.

Nat's focus flitted from Becca, who stood just out of reach, to the three people around the bed and a fourth young woman, standing at the back of the room.

"Natalie, you're all right. Thank goodness. I thought you were... you might be—"

"What's your name, dear?" The woman wearing a pinkish, floral top held a clipboard ready to take down Nat answers.

"Georgie," Nat recalled the young woman's name who stood in the corner.

"Your name is Georgie?" The nurse repeated, sounding confused. She'd exchanged concerned glances with the other nurses and posed the question again. "Can you tell me your name?"

"Natalie. My name's Natalie." Nat pulled her gaze from Georgie and looked at the nurse.

"I didn't know where to go or what to do." Georgie wrung her hands and began to pace. "I was all alone. So I came back here and found you."

"Blood pressure is one fifteen over seventy-five." The male nurse reported. He clicked on a penlight and held Nat's right eye open wide.

"Where's—" Nat stopped when the light hit her eye and she blinked.

"Can you tell me your last name, honey?" the red-haired nurse asked.

"Simon?" Nat blinked, trying to get rid of the residual big, dark blotchy spot the light had left.

"Your last name is *Simon*?" Again the nurse sounded confused and glanced at the other two attending staff.

"No, no, no. *My* last name is Powell."

The man shined the light into Nat's left eye. "Pupils, normal and reactive."

"Simon?" Georgie stopped and stared at Nat. "I remember him. The guy with the curly hair. Where is he?"

"And do you know where you are?" the nurse asked. She held her clipboard close.

"I don't know," Nat answered Georgie, realizing she was talking to two people at the same time, both required different answers and neither of them were willing to wait.

"You have no idea where you are now?" The nurse scribbled some notes.

"I'm in bed, in the hospital." Nat nearly shouted at her. As if that weren't obvious—Nat had been knocked unconscious, not oblivious.

"Good. Good." The nurse seemed pleased and a bit relieved at the correct answer. "Do you remember what happened?"

"What are you doing in the hospital?" Georgie sounded genuinely concerned.

Nat concentrated, tried to remember the last thing that happened to her before waking here.

There was the Bright Room, the bright light, and seeing Mitch.

No, before that. What had happened before...

Nat took in a deep breath and said, "I don't know. I can't remember anything."

"SO... HOW ARE you feeling? Better?" Daine wasn't exactly stuttering but he could not have sounded any more awkward. It wouldn't have surprised Nat if he were sweating bullets under his newly-wrapped head bandage. "You look... look... awake. Really awake."

"I am. I'm good." Nat glanced at Georgie—a couple of hours had gone by and she was still standing in the corner. "How long was I out?"

"They didn't tell you?"

"I didn't ask." Had Nat really wanted to know? What if it had been months—although that didn't sound right. She couldn't have been out that long. But even if it had been days, that would be bad enough.

"You've been out since yesterday afternoon, about eighteen hours, I guess."

"Eighteen hours?" Nat stared at his bandage. "Your head— what happened to your—" There was something very familiar about his injury. Something she should know... something she should—

"What kind of monster did that to my brother?" It was the

first thing Georgie had said since she'd arrived. "Whoever did that should be arrested for assault and battery."

"I did that to you, didn't I?" It took her a moment to recall everything. Then Nat remembered. The frying pan. The home run.

"You did it?" Georgie gazed wide-eyed at Nat.

"It's only a couple of stitches." Daine ran his hand over his injured head. "It's okay, it doesn't really hurt. It just looks bad."

"Why would you do something like that, Natalie?" Georgie sounded close to tears.

"I'm sorry. I don't know why...." The memory of swinging the pan came into focus, amazingly vivid. "I thought... I thought...."

"I'm glad the skillet was only All-Clad and not cast iron," he said, genuinely relieved. "Really, I understand completely. You had to get out of there. I saw what was in that closet. All those pictures and—"

"Wasn't that the freakiest thing you've ever seen?" Georgie said to Daine who, of course, could not hear her.

"I could hardly believe it. I think that woman's lost it. I really feel sorry for Greg. He doesn't deserve to have a mother like that."

"*His* mother?" Georgie said.

"Greg's mother? What do you mean?" Why would Daine say that? Didn't he feel sorry for himself? "Isn't Marion your mother, too?"

"What? My mother? Oh." Daine almost visibly shuddered. "No, she isn't. She raised me but she's not my real, my biological mother.

"My mother died a year after her divorce from George Price. Mom—Marian, I've always thought of her as Mom, took me in and raised me since I was three but I'm not her son. She never told me but I guess she figured that I was Greg's half-brother plus she got a little more money for child support. I can't blame her, she did what she could to make ends meet."

The admission shook him and he, all-of-a-sudden, seemed vulnerable.

"She's always been nurturing, supportive, and loving to me except for this one time that she tried to kill me so Greg would inherit everything from our father. I guess that's not so nice." Daine looked at Nat square in the eyes. "She told the police that she recognized my car and thought I was the one behind the wheel."

"What a loony tunes." Georgie sighed.

"Marian Price?" This was a lot for Nat and she wasn't even sure she was getting it all. "How did you find all this out?"

"Detective Holland told me about her confession. He says she told them everything."

"She confessed?" This sounded so unbelievable, but then again the woman was seriously unhinged.

"That little fender bender wasn't all she'd been up to." *He* must have been confused by the love for a mother who raised him and then tried to kill him. Daine's step-mother's confession clearly worried him.

Nat waited to hear more. This news had been pretty bad. Shocking. Could it get any worse?

"She knew the night that Greg and I were going to meet with Georgette. She encouraged us to go. She said we were George Price's kids, too, and we were entitled to more than the measly ten grand that he left us."

"I was trying to be nice," Georgie complained.

"So Greg and I met with Georgette, our half-sister. It was the first time, you know. She told us she wanted to 'even things out' between all of us."

"I had them over to the house for a nice "family" dinner," Georgie explained to Nat.

Talk about dysfunctional.

"Mom told Detective Holland that she waited until we left

before using the secret passageway to sneak in and strangle Geor-gette with one of my father's scarves."

"Well, she had lived there, hadn't she?" Nat glanced at Georgie to see her reaction. "Longer than any of old George's other wives."

"She must have been married to Daddy at least thirty years ago."

"And then he married my mother after Marian. I must have spent some early childhood years there until my parents divorced."

"So you were only two or three when you lived at the Price mansion." Nat could see how he didn't remember anything about the house.

"Well, I couldn't ever remember living there." Daine looked confused. "But I must have gone exploring. The police found my fingerprints in the passage—tiny ones."

"And they threatened you? Made it sound as if you were hiding something?"

"They were trying to scare some information or a confession out of me. Except there was nothing for me to confess."

"How did they know Marian's prints were new and not from when she lived there thirty years ago?"

"I don't know, I guess they have their ways," Daine said with a shrug. "Holland didn't seem shocked that it was her."

It was a lot for Nat to take in. "So Marian Price killed Georgie."

"That witch," Georgie swore. "That murdering old witch."

Nat's gaze drifted to Georgie whose expression went from shock to pure hatred to relief at the disclosure of her murderer. She'd finally found the answer she'd been searching for.

"Marian also admitted to killing Mrs. Price Number Three and Mrs. Price Number Four," he continued, who of course, did not know that Nat had been distracted by Georgie.

"What? You're kidding?" Nat's eyes managed to widen even more as she stared back at Daine. "How?"

"She killed my mother?" Georgie whispered in an almost calm fashion. "Why that crazy murdering psycho bitch—"

"I don't know. Holland didn't go into the details. I think the police got way more than they bargained for. They found Georgette's killer plus another two murder confessions." Daine scratched his whiskered face. "It's hard for me to believe. She was always so nice to me. I had no idea she was crazy."

15

"I'M SO GLAD you could make it for dinner." Alice opened the door of her home wide and Nat stepped inside. "It was nice of your sister to bring you here."

"I think she was willing to do just about anything to get me out of the house." Nat smiled to let Alice know that she was making a joke.

"Two *frigging* days I had to stay there!" Georgie huffed and walked through the walls into the room. "I'm just glad to get out of that hovel."

There were good points about Georgie being invisible. Nat didn't have to make excuses for her rudeness.

"Have a seat, will you?" Alice closed the front door. "I want you to remember that just because you're out and about doesn't mean you're fully recovered."

"Alice," Nat eased onto the couch and replied in a calm tone. "Your nurse is showing."

"I can't help it." She held up her hands in defeat. "I've been in full rehabilitation mode since Daine's been staying with us. I'm not sure I can turn it off."

Nat chuckled then added awkwardly. "I'm sorry to hear about Greg's mother."

"Greg's so tired of talking about it." The slight sag in Alice's shoulders told Nat it was affecting her, too. "To the detectives, the lawyers, the psychiatrist, and the other doctors. There are reporters hanging out at his office. Of course, the police are telling him not to say a word, and he hasn't. Who would want to tell the world their mother's crazy?"

"Crazy? That woman was deranged." Georgie went on. "Is there a word worse than that? If there is, she's that, too."

"It's bad enough she killed Georgette but George Price's two other wives." Alice met Nat's gaze.

"She murdered my mother." Georgie cried out, and Nat was again relieved that she couldn't be heard.

"Marian's really gone off the deep end. I never saw any signs of it, but I guess it must have always been there. I don't know when it happened but it must have been a long while ago."

"But she seemed so nice." Nat had never thought insanity could look so normal.

"She told Greg that she got the idea when Daine's mother died in a car accident. Marian said she could arrange for accidents to happen too."

So she thought she'd play God.

"She worked at Valley Central Hospital when the third Mrs. Price came in for a facelift," Alice continued. "Marian added her own special cocktail to the IV, Mrs. Price Number Three never woke from the anesthesia."

"That woman is so sick," Georgie's firm statement still held contempt for the woman.

That was a good advertisement not to have elective surgery.

"When Mrs. Price Number Four was having breast augmentation, she suffered a heart attack the day after surgery."

Perky boobs were not worth it.

"She was keeping her husband happy by looking the best she could." Georgie defended her mother.

"Greg was understandably upset when she confessed. He's standing by her and making sure she's getting the care she needs."

"The police aren't going to charge her with murder, are they? They can't, she's—" Nat left *nuts* unsaid.

"I'd appreciate it if you don't talk about this when Greg's around."

"I won't." Nat wasn't sure how one would bring up the subject of a mass-murdering mother.

"Well, I'm not about to keep quiet about it!" Georgie complained. "That wicked witch killed me *and* my mother. I want justice. I want—"

"Where is Greg?" Nat did her best to ignore Georgie's raving. "And where's Daine?"

"Greg took Daine shopping. Apparently, we don't have the right *ingredients* for dinner. He mumbled something about how the steaks I bought weren't fit for human consumption and that we need some fresh something-or-other that I didn't have and then off he went, dragging Greg along as chauffeur."

Nat thought about making excuses for Daine, about being a hot-headed, temperamental chef and all but he was Alice's brother-in-law. She must have already known that when it came to food and cooking, he had a nasty temper.

"We're not holding to the professional-chefs-don't-cook dinner rule in this household." Alice chuckled. "Greg and I are counting on it. If I have to cook dinner you can bet I'll have to pump your stomachs for dessert."

"Did he say anything about dessert?"

"He didn't get that far. He told me to tell you to be inventive and whip something up when you got here."

Wasn't that just like him? Bark out cooking orders and then leave.

Nat stood and motioned Alice to lead on. "Let's go into the kitchen and see what you have stocked."

"I'm staying here," Georgie sobbed. She collapsed onto the couch where Nat had sat moments before. "I can't believe my mother was murdered by the same woman who killed me."

Nat wished Simon was around to comfort Georgie. She couldn't stay. Where had Simon gone, by the way? Nat took one last glance over her shoulder at Georgie before stepping into the next room.

"Where do we start?" Alice stood next to the granite island in the center of the kitchen, ready to work.

It would depend on what they were going to make. And Nat had no idea. There were some necessities needed in any case. They could start there.

"I guess we'll need some basic things. Some big bowls and a mixer would be nice."

"I've got a measuring cup and some measuring spoons," Alice said brightly.

Nat could always eyeball measurements but she wasn't about to turn down any kind of equipment. "Do you have a food processor?"

Alice glanced at the wall cabinets as if she had x-ray vision and could see their contents. "I don't think so, but I'll check."

Didn't Alice know? This was her kitchen, wasn't it?

Rummaging through the fridge and cabinets, Nat found some ingredients she could use, flour, sugar, butter, and eggs. Among the decorative eggplant and artichoke centerpiece on the dining room table were a few lemons that were in fairly decent shape. She grabbed those, too. She pulled out a large zip-top bag, a box of aluminum foil and a low, square dish that she could use for a traybake.

Alice stood at the island next to her finds which were a couple of mixing bowls and a small box.

"A hand mixer is all you have?" It was brand new, the box looked as if it had never been opened.

"You're lucky I have that." Alice stared at the box as if trying to remember something about it. "I think it was a wedding present."

Nat didn't want to break the news to Alice, but whipping egg whites into meringue with a hand mixer would take next to forever. On the other hand, it would keep Alice busy.

Alice, with mixer at the ready, stood at a bowl containing four egg whites. Nat told her to add the sugar that she'd placed in a coffee mug a little at a time. She crossed her fingers that this would work without cream of tartar. Nat felt there was a very slim chance she'd find that ingredient here.

"Just keep beating them until they turn into a thick white foam." Nat busied herself by cutting the flour and butter drizzling in some iced water. Then she dropped in some vegetable shortening until the mixture turned crumbly.

"What are you doing?" Georgie appeared out of thin air and scared Nat. She turned, lost her balance, and cried out, causing the bowl to slide off the counter. Her quick reflexes, caught it before it crashed to the ground.

"What did you say?" Alice called out to Nat over the drone of her mixer.

"Just working on the pie crust," Nat replied, answering both of them. With enough elbow grease, anything is possible. Nearly anything, anyway.

Alice still worked on the egg whites. Nat placed her dough mixture in the large, plastic zip-top bag. She kneaded and squeezed the mixture into a ball then pressed it flat before popping it into the fridge.

"How's that meringue coming?" She called to Alice while she washed her hands.

"Still working on it," Alice yelled back. They were both going to sound hoarse by the time they were finished.

"Don't give up, it'll thicken," Nat encouraged. As she said, it was going to take near-forever.

Over medium heat, Nat combined lemon juice, sugar, and egg yolks in a saucepan.

Georgie leaned into the pot to see what was cooking. "Oh, that's nasty. It's all raw and gooey."

Nat rolled her eyes and ignored her. She kept stirring the lemon filling until it bubbled then turned off the heat and allowed it to cool.

"Any progress?" Nat checked on Alice's egg whites.

"They're foamy." Alice tilted the mixer to one side of the bowl to let Nat see the contents. "Don't you think?"

"You're getting there." Nat sprinkled in more sugar to help thicken it up. "It'll turn into meringue any minute now."

Georgie took Nat's place when she stepped away and took a look for herself. "Eww. That's goo, too."

Nat would bet that Georgie didn't know how to boil water. She probably thought raw tap water was gross.

Nat pulled a bottle of wine from a rack off the counter.

"Is that for us?" A smile flickered on Alice's overtaxed face.

"Sorry, I'm not opening this." Nat wiped the bottle with a dish towel before wrapping it with her all-purpose aluminum foil and dusting it with flour. Without a rolling pin, she had to make do with what she had.

"I thought you were going to drink that." Georgie drawled through lowered lids. "I know I would."

Nat couldn't begin to make Georgie understand the delicate science of crust making, and wasn't even going to try. How a square pie was going to turn out, Nat had no idea. She used the wine bottle to roll the pie crust flat.

"Isn't that tedious?" Georgie and Alice chorused as they watched Nat work with the dough.

And there was a moment of silence. Odd silence. It seemed the motor from the mixer went dead and the fan from the preheating oven quieted. Then the DING from the oven sounded, indicating it had finished preheating, bringing back the flow of normal time.

Nat flipped the crust into the square dish. "Not at all." She glanced from Georgie to Alice, thinking how odd it was they'd said the exact same thing at the exact same time.

She took the foil from the wine bottle and pressed it over the crust.

Georgie stared at Alice. She was the only one of them to hear the repetition.

Nat reached for one of the decorative canisters filled with pinto beans and poured half the contents onto the foil in the baking dish, pressing the beans into the edges.

"What's happened?" Georgie's voice sounded uncertain. "Something weird is happening. *Nat-a-lie*."

Nat slid the pie crust into the oven to bake. If something supernatural was going on, she didn't know anything about it.

"HAVE I TOLD you that I hate that hat?" The very familiar words, once spoken by Mitch Hudson, were uttered unmistakably by Daine.

She turned her head toward Georgie and they stared wide-eyed at one another for a good five seconds. They were still in the kitchen and the major creep factor penetrated both their realities.

"Mitch used to say that." Georgie was the first to say it out loud. It had been the exact same thing Nat had been thinking.

"You heard Alice." Greg sounded as if they were trying to be the voice of reason. "She said you looked like the walking wounded without it."

"This thing is driving me crazy. I'm taking this stupid bandage off."

The sound of rustling bags, both paper and plastic, and the *THUNK* they made hitting the floor must have been the groceries the men had purchased. Alice powered down her mixer and set it on the counter, stalking toward the door, ready to confront the whole "bandage issue."

"You *will* leave it on." Alice stood in the doorway and ordered in an authoritative nurse's voice. One that no one who knew what was good for them would disobey. "It doesn't matter if you like it or not. You're going to wear that until the doctor gives the okay to remove it. Is that clear?"

Nat and Georgie stood a good two feet behind Alice and peered into the living room over her shoulder. Daine glanced at Greg, who narrowed his eyes to warn his brother not to cross his wife by even thinking about doing away with his bandage.

The timer went off and Nat rushed to the oven to pull out the crust. She ran right back to the living room in time to see Alice doing her best to keep Daine, who was putting up a pretty good fight, from tearing the gauze from his head.

"But it's a wonderful shade of blue, it matches your eyes." Alice was winning the battle.

"All right. Stop—all right." Daine stopped struggling and held his hands up in surrender. "I don't care if it's blue, it's dog-ugly."

Nat had stepped into the living room and got a good look at Daine. Not only had he shaved the stubble on his cheeks and jawline since the last time she saw him, he had shaved off his goatee.

He stood there completely clean-shaven.

"He has a dimple right in the middle of his chin, just like Mitch." Georgie again echoed Nat's very thoughts.

And so he had. She stared at him.

"You're here," Daine said to Nat. Every ounce of hostility he'd only moments before exuded had vanished. He smiled, genuinely happy to see her.

"You're a man bearing groceries, I see." Nat grabbed the handles on a couple of bags, helping out, but she couldn't take her eyes off the cleft in his chin.

"I've been locked up here for days." Daine picked up a couple more bags and backed into the kitchen. "I couldn't stand it anymore. I needed the sweet smell of fresh produce in an open-air market."

"You said it, brother." Georgie heaved a heavy sigh.

Nat knew exactly what they both meant.

"I think Nat likes your new look." A knowing smile spread over Alice's face.

Daine set his bag on the counter and ran his hand over his smooth jaw. He glanced at Nat and seemed pleased that it had pleased her.

"What's happening here?" Nat whispered, not sure exactly what she meant, but something had changed. This was a Daine Nat hadn't seen before, and it was more than just his newly discovered cleft chin and his bright blue turban. There was something different about him.

"My mug was so hairy, I decided to take it all off."

His *mug*?

That was a weird thing to say. Not language anyone nowadays used.

"You like it, huh?" One side of Daine's mouth hitched into a smile. "If I'd have known that I would have shaved it off a long time ago."

16

THEN AN IDEA came to her... and a whole different way of thinking.

Georgie had thought they were here to help her find her murderer, sort of an after-death CSI investigation. But as it turned out, it wasn't that at all.

Yes, they'd found her killer. Yes, they'd uncovered two additional murders. It wasn't until now that Georgie realized that wasn't really the point—not directly. Solving her death was only a way to combine their efforts, to make them work together, give them something to focus on.

How could she have been so shallow and stupid?

Hadn't that been the way it always was? Not at all what she was used to. Everything had always revolved around Georgie, or so she had thought anyway. Her father and her friends. Didn't Georgie believe she was the center of the world? Why would anything change after her death? She didn't think it would.

Did her friends Liz and Dahlia still care for her? Above all, they had thought of her first. Weren't the police tearing the house apart for clues, looking for the murderer? Hadn't she been front-page news for a week? It seemed as if the whole world had cared.

Why wouldn't she believe all this had been for her benefit? Even after death, those around her had considered her and her wishes.

She'd thought that all along. Until just a few minutes ago when she'd seen her brothers, Greg and Daine. But they weren't the same now as they were before. She hadn't really known them, but the three of them were related. Glimpsing them through fresh eyes, she decided that they had changed. They were familiar yet somehow different.

There were bits of Mitch in Daine, from the odd use of words down to the newly revealed dimple in his chin. Had it been her imagination that she saw elements of Simon in Greg? Greg who was in bad need of a bedside manner transplant, got one similar to with empathetic Simon? Was that possible?

After all, this life and beyond stuff was all new to Georgie. She didn't know the rules or how things were supposed to work. But it had to be possible, didn't it? Couldn't it?

This wasn't about her after all. It was about realizing what your problems were during your life and fixing them. The three of them coming together had been about Mitch's and Simon's moving on, not about Georgie at all. She had only helped.

And although she was alive, Natalie had to play some part in all this. She had seen and was shocked by the changes in her brothers as well. Was this paranormal episode in her life meant to somehow change it?

If Natalie were to change her life from here on out and both Mitch and Simon had already moved on—Georgie didn't want to sound self-centered again and bring this back to her, but what about her? Where was she to go and what was to happen to her?

Did Georgie deserve another chance?

17

THERE'S NOTHING MORE formidable than seeing a man in a blue turban with a knife. If he were the wrong man, he could use the knife as a weapon. If he were the right man, he could use the same knife for whittling ingredients into bite-sized pieces and create an amazing meal.

Daine stood next to the granite-topped island, overseeing the flurry of culinary activity going on around him. With a dozen or so quick, easy strokes, he sliced a tomato, then with a quarter turn, he cut again, dicing it before sliding it off the cutting board into a bowl. Then did two more before handing the bowl to Greg.

"We can have only one person in charge today and that's going to be me," Daine announced.

"Don't bug him," Alice whispered to Nat. "He's in his element."

And in one of his infamous *Maestro of the Meal* moods, Nat almost added. That's how the old kitchen staff referred to him behind his back. Daine acted as if he were conducting the Philadelphia Symphonic Orchestra through Beethoven's Fifth Symphony instead of giving food instruction in a kitchen.

"Can you help me with this?" Greg fumbled with a garlic press and turned to Daine who still stood near the island. Greg pulled the handle open and the plump clove fell onto the obviously-brand-new cutting board. "I can't figure out how you're supposed to—"

In a flash, Daine covered the garlic with the wide part of his knife and smashed the blade with his fist, flattening the garlic. He scraped the garlic pulp onto his knife and dropped it into Greg's palm.

"O-kay." Greg stood inert, staring at the odiferous pulp. "I think that'll do."

"Do you need something else?" Daine asked his brother. "You have a comment to make, maybe?"

"Who me?" Greg stepped back, returning to his stovetop. "I'm a lowly kitchen peon. I wouldn't dream of making a suggestion about something I know nothing about. You are the Master Chef, little brother."

Nat snickered to herself.

And no one better forget it.

"Are these soft peaks?" Alice had turned off the mixer and lifted the beaters from the egg whites.

"Not yet, keep whipping," Daine barked before Nat could answer.

"Hey, you told us that dessert was our area." Nat scolded him. "This isn't Sam's kitchen, you can't order us around. You just keep tabs on your entrée on your side."

"Sam's kitchen or not, if we want to eat on time, we've got to keep to a schedule, *doll*."

Nat spun around to stare at him. "What did you just call me?"

"I said..." Daine stopped. "Are you going to finish dessert on time or not?"

A cell phone rang. He reached into his pocket and pulled out his phone. "This is Daine." A pause. He looked at Nat. "Yeah. Just a sec." He held out his cell to her. "It's Becca."

"Hello?" Nat stole a look at Daine from the corner of her eye. There was something about the crinkle of his eye, just in the corner, and the curve of the edge of his mouth that reminded her of Mitch.

"Becca? Why are you calling me on Daine's phone?"

"Because you're not answering yours and this is too important to leave a message."

"Sorry, I'm in the kitchen and my phone's in the other room." A quick glance to the living room reminded Nat where she had left her purse containing her cell phone. What she really wanted to know was how he and Becca became close enough to be on a cell-phone-number-swapping basis. "How did you get this number?"

"Daine gave it to me at the hospital, when we were at your bedside vigil."

So it was as innocent as that. Nat scoffed at herself. "I just thought it was weird. That's all."

"You're not jealous are you?" Becca chuckled. "Do you think I'm trying to move in on your man?"

"He's not—" Nat didn't go on and glanced at him to see if he had any idea that they were talking about him. She hoped she wasn't blushing. Just the thought of Daine belonging to her or them being....

"I just had to tell you that when I got home—there's a phone message from—" Becca said with a once-upon-a-time tone. "I had to call and tell you. I didn't think you wanted to wait until tomorrow to hear. I knew you'd be seeing Daine, and I had his cell number so—"

If the message was so important, why hadn't they called her cell number? Maybe they did. Maybe they'd called and she left her purse in the other room. "Will you stop talking and just tell me, already?"

"You got a call from Side Street Sam's, they're offering you the position!" Becca shrieked. "That's so great, isn't it?"

"What?" It was all Nat could do not to jump up and down and scream with joy at the top of her lungs. "Oh, my gosh—you're kidding. You're not kidding are you?" She glanced at Greg, Alice, and Daine who all looked expectantly back at her. "You'd better not be kidding because it wouldn't be funny."

"I wouldn't joke about something like this. I know how important this is to you. You go ahead and ask Daine. I'm sure he must know all about it."

"Is it true?" Nat shifted the attention focused on her to him. "Side Street Sam's wants me?"

"I didn't want to spoil the surprise." He was Mr. Calm, Cool, and Collected. Of course, he knew and he had kept quiet about the news.

"Oh, my gosh." The truth soaked into Nat. She didn't jump around with enthusiasm. She stood there shocked.

Daine pulled his cell from Nat's hand. "Natalie can't talk right now. Thanks for passing on the good news, Becca." A pause. "Uh-huh. Okay. Later." He hung up.

"You're going to work at Sam's? With Daine?" Greg didn't sound so much shocked or happy as much as confused by Nat's news. "You *want* to work with him?"

"I didn't think I'd get the job." Nat managed. "I never thought.... You already knew, didn't you?"

Daine shrugged. "You'll be a great addition to the staff. I think you've got some real talent. Who knows, maybe you can even teach me a thing or two."

Nat would never count on that happening. "Hey!" She pointed at Alice's egg whites. They had turned into meringue. "Okay, stop already. You're done."

"Finally." Alice sighed. "If I'm ever going to do this again I want a bigger mixer, one that I don't have to hold up for three hours."

"Oh, come on now. It wasn't *that* bad." Nat waved at Alice to put the hand mixer down. "Next you're going to take your meringue and spread it over the top of the lemon curd."

"Me? Why do I have to do it?" Alice took the rubber spatula Nat held out to her.

"I don't think I can grip the handle." She held out her hands and showed how they were trembling with excitement. "I'd end up dropping the bowl, the pie, or maybe both."

"Oh, no you don't." Alice grew protective and moved closer to the counter. She wasn't going to let Nat near anything. "Not after all that work I did to whip those eggs. I'm not going to chance losing our dessert."

The front door buzzer sounded. "I'll get it." Greg left the kitchen while Nat talked Alice through topping off the lemon pie with raw meringue and Daine looked on.

By the time the pie had been popped into the oven for its fifteen minutes, Greg had returned to the kitchen. He held a good-sized box marked with a big Eyewitness KPIX TV logo.

"Daine, it's for you." Greg set the box on the island where his brother stood.

"Well, what do you know?" Daine said, mildly surprised. He took the box and slit it open with the single blade of the kitchen scissors. He lifted the lid, peered inside, and smiled.

"And this is my good news." He reached into the box. "I've been offered my own weekend cooking program." He pulled out a dark blue baseball hat and set it on his head. The front read: *The Great Daine* in a stylish, swirly script.

"A TV show?" There was a curious inflection in Greg's voice. Not that he was jealous. He sounded impressed, star struck, even.

"The director said that my segment went great," Daine began. "I'm no Alton Brown or anything, but when the piece aired I somehow... 'leaped off the screen,' to use his words." He held his hand up as to hold off the harsh criticism he knew would come from those related to him. "He said the phone calls lit up their switchboard. Then there were the emails and letters—the feedback was phenomenal. The audience, the TV people, they loved me. And it's funny because I've been on television before and I've never had a response anything near that."

So he had instant *man*-gnetisim.

"And now they're giving you your own show." Alice stood there nearly open-mouthed.

"Yeah, that's right." Daine stood there with his head held high, as if soaking in the words of admiration from an invisible auditorium filled with his hundreds, maybe thousands, of equally invisible, adoring fans.

"I thought your dream was to open your own restaurant?" Greg turned away from the cooktop.

"That's still the plan."

"There are only two of us splitting the Price fortune now. You should get more than enough to open your restaurant." Greg laughed. "You can have one in every state. You can have a whole chain of them if you want."

"One'll be enough. I don't know. We'll see. I'll think about it after the estate is settled. There's time." Daine caught sight of Greg's empty skillet. "What's going on with our dinner?"

"Huh?" Greg was so busy with his inheritance talk, he must have forgotten about his current task.

"And I don't know about you but I'm getting hungry," Daine complained. "If you don't get cooking, we don't eat."

"I'm on it." Greg gestured with his slotted spoon. "Don't worry, I've got it all under control."

"Have you?" Daine pointed at Greg's empty pan. "I see a bunch of nothing going on there."

"I'm working on it. See—" He motioned to the prepped raw ingredients next to him, waiting to be made into dinner. "I'm getting my stuff all chopped up and standing by, just like you told me. I'll be ready for step two soon."

"You'd better pay attention when it comes to the cooking part because the meat cooks up fast." Daine stepped closer to keep an eye on his brother. "First, set the burner on medium heat."

Greg turned the knob and glanced under the skillet at the flame.

"After you've heated up the pan, add a little olive oil. Swirl the oil to coat the bottom of the pan. Now toss in the onions and crushed garlic. Let it simmer in the pan for a minute, maybe two, then add the meat."

Greg pushed the onions and garlic around the pan with his spoon. The aroma filled the kitchen. Daine gave him the go-ahead to add the meat and the delicious sizzle sounded.

"I think I'll make up a little *au jus* here, for our sandwiches, just to top them off." Daine pulled out a copper saucepan from a shopping bag and washed it by hand at the sink. It wasn't from the non-stick Circulon set Alice and Greg owned.

Nat guessed it might be an All-Clad or Raffoni. It wouldn't have surprised her that he bought a special pot for one-time use. He was, after all, an artist, and temperamental when it came to cooking. He placed his pot on the burner next to Greg's skillet. There, Daine could simmer and keep an eye on his brother.

He added some of this and a little of that to his pot and stirred it with great care. "I've decided to take your advice, Alice," he said. "I'm putting together a collection of my sauce recipes in a book. I thought I'd call it *It's All Gravy* unless you can come up with a better title."

Alice smiled and with a nod of her head must have thought that her brother-in-law was one okay guy. "I'll have to give that some thought."

The front door buzzed again.

"I'll get it." Alice left and returned minutes later. "It's from the auction. You know, Greg, the one I told you about where the proceeds go to the Children's Hospital?"

A children's hospital auction? That sounded familiar. Where had Nat heard of that?

Alice sliced the tape with the blade with the same pair of scissors Daine had used for his box. "Isn't this the best purse you've ever seen?" She held up what looked like a gargantuan fig with a bunch of gold-colored chains hanging from it.

"It's big, but not too big." She held it up to show its size. "And it's got all these dividers and tons of pockets to put stuff in. And a special compartment for your cell phone and keys."

Nat noticed Daine and Greg's eyes widened in surprise. It seemed that they were just as shocked to hear those words coming from Alice. But Nat had heard those exact words before—from Georgie.

It couldn't be Georgie's purse. Nat was sure that there couldn't be another purse that ugly in existence.

"May I have a look at that?" Nat reached out for the bag which Alice willingly handed to her.

"You see." Alice sniffed at the boys with almost a snobbish air. "Natalie knows quality when she sees it."

And since when was Alice all girly-girly? And when had she started...called her *Natalie*?

"Thanks," Nat flipped the clasp open and pulled the stem of the fig up, looking into the bag.

'In the bottom' Georgie had said. The secret pocket, that's where she'd kept her emergency platinum card.

Nat ran her finger around the bottom lining. She felt it-the familiar shape of a credit card. She searched for the pocket opening.

Tucking her finger inside the opening Nat knew was there, she coaxed the midnight blue plastic card with its silver-colored card holder's name and numbers from its place. She made out the name *Georgette Price* then slid the card back.

"It's some prize, all right." Nat snapped the purse closed and handed it back to Alice. "You must feel very lucky to have won it."

"Who else would want that?" Daine used a snarl that was usually reserved for incompetent kitchen staff, not directed at his sister-in-law. "Greg, what do you think? You're not going to let her keep something like that in the house, are you?"

"As long as she loves it, that's all that matters," Greg said in an uncharacteristic, understanding way. What had happened to the doctor without the bedside manner?

Nat looked at the three of them. What was going on? She was looking at a brusque Daine, a kind, un-opinionated Greg, and now a purse-loving Alice?

Nat thought that Georgie was the only one who loved.... Where *had* Georgie gone?

"Excuse me." Nat headed out of the kitchen for the living room. She peeked out the door, took a good look around, and in an urgent whisper called out, "Georgie? Georgie? Are you still here?"

She wasn't. Nat knew, yes, *knew* that she was alone. There were no more voices. No more dead people following her. Could it be? She could hardly believe it. Was all this over?

Still, Nat couldn't help but wonder where they were. She'd grown to care about them. Even for spoiled little rich girl Georgie.

Nat returned to the kitchen, her eyes a little moist.

"Come over here, *doll*," Daine called to her. "You taste this and tell me that it's not the best thing you've ever eaten."

Doll? Mitch used to call her that. Nat looked up at Daine. This *was* Daine but he had some characteristics of Mitch. In an expression or the way he looked at her or in the all-of-a-sudden way he called her *doll*.

This was Daine and Mitch, somehow had they become one.

"Greg, tell her what you think." Daine ordered and immediately said, "He thinks it's fantastic."

"I wouldn't dare try to sway her with my opinion." Greg turned his back to them and found a sudden interest in the food sizzling in his pan.

Nat took the spoon from Daine, touched it to her lips to taste, and let her taste buds decide. It was delicious, rich, warm, and fairly complex. It would be a good complement to beef, but....

"It's good." She shrugged at Alice then looked at Daine. But it wasn't his usual make-you-weak-at-the-knees good. "I know you outrank me in the kitchen, but you know what would make this out of this world?"

"What?" He sounded more curious than outraged. That surprised her. A critique of his cooking normally made him blow a fuse.

"You think you can make Daine's savory sauce better?" Alice dove into the gravy with her own spoon. Maybe she was checking to see if it were possible that he made some sub-standard sauce.

"What you need is a touch of soy sauce. Not too much, I think just a teaspoon, maybe a teaspoon and a half."

Daine stepped to the range, between Nat and his pot. He stared into his sauce and stirred. She could see he was doing some quick mental taste tests—a little culinary chemistry. He held out his hand and called out, "Soy sauce."

Alice slapped the bottle in his palm as if it were medical equipment during a surgical procedure.

Daine eyeballed a teaspoon then a dash more before stirring it smooth. They tasted it and shifted his gaze to Nat. "You're good."

He placed his spoon on the rest and pulled her into his arms. Nat caught the intensity in his face, his eyes.

"Maybe we're better together as a team," he said.

This felt right. She wanted this.

The oven timer buzzed and Alice called to Nat. "Does that mean it's ready?"

Daine had to tell Alice to pull the pie out of the oven. Nat was totally out of it. She couldn't care less if the meringue on the pie had burned.

"We're a natural complementary pairing and I'm not talking about food." He bent his head to kiss her.

He was right. If Nat had learned anything maybe it was there was more to life than just food.

Who cared about dinner? Who cared about pie?

Nat wrapped her arms around Daine's neck and kissed him back.

About the Author

California-born Shirley Marks lives in Silicon
Valley with her husband and unpredictable
Australian Cattle Dog-mix.

Shirley dreams of returning to London, Paris,
and Florence to research settings, develop new
characters, and stories to weave together for
her upcoming novels.

When at home, she spends time reading,
writing, gardening, and trying to get the odd
knitting projects completed

Shirley writes Traditional Regency Romance
stories (clean/sweet), Romantic Comedies,
and a couple of paranormal novels

You can visit Shirley at:
www.ShirleyMarks.com